FOUR WEDDINGS AND A MURDER

A FIONA MCCABE MYSTERY

KATHY CRANSTON

"I never said I wanted to be involved in a wedding planning business. What's the matter, did you have wax in your ears when I asked you to help me set up as a private investigator?"

Fiona McCabe looked up and was taken aback by the mutinous fury on her grandmother's face.

But that was the least of her worries.

"Granny Coyle, for the love of God can you help me with this?"

"With what? Sure how can I help you? We can't both beat those eggs. That'd be the height of stupidity."

"I don't know." Exasperated, Fiona brushed her hair away from her forehead with her arm. Her hands were covered in a sugary egg mixture that seemed to have the sticking power of glue. She didn't have time for this. "Maybe you can roll out that pastry?"

Rose Coyle set her mouth and moved as far away from the counter as it was possible to get in the small kitchen.

It had all started a few months back. Fiona had been minding her own business running the pub and attempting to extract some sort of a living from it when her granny had approached her with a new business idea.

She could see the sense in it—sort of. After all, they'd just tracked down a murderer and she supposed there was a level of pride to take in that. Her granny had found it hard to go back to ordinary life after stalking around lanes and spying on suspected wrong-doers.

So Fiona had relented after a bit of arm-twisting.

It turned out she needn't have worried. The process of becoming a licensed PI in Ireland was so convoluted that she doubted she'd have to worry much more about it for at least another year.

She'd been delighted.

She hadn't admitted that of course. Not to her granny and not to the rest of her family, who'd no doubt relish the opportunity of telling tales on her to their granny. Everyone was afraid of Granny Coyle. Even the local Garda Sergeant.

Fiona hadn't banked on her sister Kate's inability to manage her finances. No sooner had Granny Coyle accepted that the PI thing might have to wait a while than Kate was approaching Fi with a business proposal of her own. She'd maxed out her credit card buying makeup and hair products online and their parents had finally seen sense and refused to bail her out.

So she was going to set up a wedding planning business to help get her finances in order.

Which seemed sensible. It even seemed like she was turning a corner. She'd managed to convince the Credit Union to give her a loan to get set up.

This was all well and good until Fiona discovered Kate had registered her pub as the business address. And it wasn't just on paper: the little snug in the pub soon became Kate's headquarters.

The beauty of Kate's plan was that it was so outlandish her older sister hadn't taken it seriously. And by the time Fiona began to see that Kate *was* serious, it was far too late to argue. In hindsight, Kate taking over the snug had been the least of her worries.

Fiona was looking around for another task to

dole out to her grandmother when something struck her.

She popped her head out of the tiny kitchen behind the bar. They weren't going to use that kitchen to cater the event of course—they'd made an agreement with the restaurant across the road to use their kitchen. The restaurant hadn't yet closed for the evening so they'd started working on the desserts in the pub kitchen.

Well, technically Kate was supposed to be working on the desserts. Fiona had a pub to run. Granny Coyle had Sudoku puzzles to work on. Even Mrs Davis from the shop next door had plonked herself down at the bar and was busy making little flowers out of icing.

Fiona gritted her teeth. "Where's Kate?"

Granny Coyle stopped her grumbling in response to the unmistakeable menace in Fiona's tone. "I don't know. I haven't seen her since your mother shooed us all out from under her feet."

Fi shook her head unable to believe it. She threw off her apron and stormed to the back of the pub, almost knocking over the ladder on which her brother Marty was perched hanging gold paper streamers off the light fittings.

She thundered up the stairs and into her flat.

The little living area was empty. She was about to turn around and march back downstairs when she heard voices coming from her bedroom.

Sure enough, her sister was sprawled on the bed, shoes still on, phone in hand.

"What the hell are you doing in here?"

Laughing, Kate finally took her eyes off her phone and shook her head. "Have you seen the latest episode of Sam's Stories on YouTube? It's gas, Fi. You should watch it."

"Oh should I, Kate? Well, I can't. I'm busy making desserts." She stormed forward and grabbed one of the cushions from behind her sister. "For. This. Damn. Wedding. Of. Yours. Tomorrow." She punctuated each word by slamming the cushion into her sister's face.

"Ow, Fi! What are you doing? Have you gone mad? I'm telling Mam."

"You can't," Fi said, dropping the cushion. "She's busy. Cleaning up after your mess."

"What mess?"

"Please tell me you haven't forgotten about the wedding here tomorrow? You planned it. You took their deposit to secure the booking without asking me."

"I... I..." Kate's eyes filled with tears. "I was just

trying to make my own way in the world. I thought you'd be proud of me."

Fi's eyes narrowed. She was good, there was no denying that. Some of Kate's performances were Oscar-worthy. Even Fi felt a fleeting burst of guilt right then.

Fleeting.

She knew her sister too well to fall for it.

"You couldn't care less what anybody thinks of you. Admit it. You're lazy. Why bother doing the work if you can get somebody else to do it, right?"

A slow, easy smile spread itself across Kate's face, which was suspiciously dry for someone who'd had such a rush of emotions just a moment earlier. "Sure I was delegating. You and Mam were only too willing to do the work. I'm a manager. I'm not the CEO of McCabe Weddings for nothing."

"Get the hell downstairs before I call these brides and tell them the venue's been cancelled."

Kate narrowed her eyes. "You wouldn't do that."

"Try me."

"You wouldn't. How could you be so vindictive? You'd ruined someone's big day?"

"No, *you'd* ruin their big days. You ruined them by making promises you knew you could never deliver on. I cannot believe you suckered four grown women into signing you on as their wedding planner."

Kate smiled triumphantly. "See? I don't need to do the grunt work. I'm the sales and marketing brains behind this operation."

She picked up her phone as if that was the end of the matter. The sound of YouTube videos filled the little room again.

Fiona wrenched the phone from her sister and threw it at the wall, where it fell apart.

Kate stared at her aghast. "What did you do that for?"

"What do you think? Now, get downstairs and find an apron."

"But I need my phone to run my business! You idiot!"

She jumped up off the bed, picked up the pieces and hurried out of the room, no doubt heading straight for the landline in the pub to call their mother and tell them what a meanie Fiona was being.

Fi didn't care.

The phone would be fine. It wasn't the first time she'd fired a phone at that wall. Her sanity on the other hand? Well, that was debatable.

Trust Kate. Their mother had tried to console Fi

that the wedding business probably wasn't going to take off anyway, but Fi had to hand it to her younger sister—she'd done something right. Within a few weeks of setting up the website and annoying all her friends to share her Facebook posts and Instagram snaps, she'd lined up her first client.

And then her second.

And third.

And fourth.

Which might have been fine, if she hadn't scheduled them all within a two week period.

That was why Fiona was in such an uncharacteristically foul mood.

The first wedding was the next day.

And it wasn't like they could chill out after all their hard work.

Because once it was over, they had less than two days to turn the pub around for the next event.

Which they were catering...

MCing...

Bartending...

Decorating...

And probably a lot of other things Kate hadn't even told them about yet.

Yes, Kate McCabe had a lot to answer for—if her

siblings weren't too exhausted to get revenge on her in two weeks' time when they finally got their lives back.

2

They had hurried across the road laden down with bags and boxes as soon as the owner of the restaurant called to say she was finished up for the night. It was nine now and they were nowhere near finished. It wasn't a particularly big crowd—the party was for fifty guests—but it would be a hard task to do all that prep work even with the use of the restaurant kitchen.

The last thing they were expecting was company.

There was a tap-tap noise on the window. They'd been working in silence, focusing all their attention on the work at hand. Fi was preparing the marinade for the lamb. Their mother was making the sauce for the chicken. Kate was half-heartedly chopping whatever vegetables could be prepared in advance and stored in the fridge for the next day.

Fi looked up, assuming it was Granny Coyle coming back to help them after her game of bridge.

But it wasn't her grandmother. Rose Coyle didn't tend to purse her lips like a cat's behind, for one thing. For another, Fi couldn't remember ever seeing her granny wearing a full face of makeup. The only light outside the window was a solar-powered sensor light, which was obviously weak given Ireland's almost total lack of sun. Even so, it was clear that the woman standing outside was rouged to within an inch of her life.

"Ah no," Mrs McCabe sighed. "Not that one again."

It was Mrs Fintan Flanagan.

Kate had assured them that pub weddings would be no bother. After all, only a low-key bride would choose such a venue. They'd believed her because it made sense. None of them had considered the possibility of a demanding mother of the bride who vocally disapproved of her daughter's choice of venue.

"I'll go see what she wants," Fi said, taking off her apron and hurrying to the door just as Mrs Flanagan looked set to tap the window again with a ruby red talon. "How did she even find us?"

"I dunno," Kate muttered. "It's like she has eyes

at the back of her head and supersonic hearing. I'm sure she's a witch."

"Kate!"

"It's true, Mammy. I swear. I wouldn't say such a thing lightly."

"In that case can you keep your voice down?" Fi called back with one hand on the door. "You're not exactly being subtle." She fixed a smile on her face and flung the door open. "Mrs Flanagan. What are you doing out here? The restaurant's closed for the night and this is a staff only area."

The woman pushed past her and bustled inside. "I'm not here for the restaurant. Good God almighty. This place?" She shuddered as if Fi had suggested something truly sickening.

"How can we help you so?"

It was about half nine by that stage. They still had all the starters to prepare before they could even think of going home for the night.

"That's it? That's the hospitality you're going to offer me after I agreed to pay you a fortune?"

Fi glanced at her mother and sister, neither of whom looked very happy or particularly inclined to respond. She took a deep breath and exhaled slowly. It did little to ease her irritation. "This isn't our place of business. We've hired the kitchen to prepare for a wedding tomorrow. I can't offer you food or a drink because I don't have any. Unless you'd like some raw chicken or marinating lamb?"

Cerise pink lips pursed even tighter. "I've never heard the likes of it! Are you this rude to all of your paying customers?"

At this—and probably seeing her sister's growing ire—Kate darted forward and took Mrs Flanagan's hand, holding the woman's elbow with her other hand as she shook it, like a nervous politician canvassing the day before an election.

"Mrs Flanagan! It's such a pleasure to see you. We're a bit under pressure here I'm afraid. Don't mind my sister. She's the brawn of this operation. Not the most socially adjusted, shall we say. Now, how can we help you? We could head on over to Phelan's for a nice nightcap if you'd prefer?"

Fi stared aghast. This diplomatic Kate was almost unrecognisable from her usual surly self. It was hard to believe.

"I don't want a *nice nightcap*."

"They do tea and coffee too. And sandwiches."

"I didn't drive all the way here from Dublin for some pub grub."

"I'm sure you didn't," Kate agreed. "But isn't it nice to have the option if you're hungry?"

Mrs Flanagan didn't see fit to respond. "I've been trying to contact you. What kind of wedding planner doesn't answer her telephone?"

Kate turned and glared at her older sister. It turned out not all phones could withstand being thrown against a wall. "My apologies for that. We've had a bit of a coverage outage here today. Must have been the storm."

"I've never seen a calmer day in November!"

"Well," Kate said thoughtfully. "Aren't ye lucky? It was wild as anything down here today. Trees blown down. Cars blown off the road."

Fi gritted her teeth. It was a barefaced lie. Maybe Kate hadn't changed so much after all. She couldn't hold it against her though—it was Fi's fault for breaking the phone.

"My phone works here."

"Does it?" Kate said breezily. "That's great. Maybe mine is working again too."

Mrs Flanagan glowered at her. "That's all you've got to say? After I driving all the way down here? You're an ignorant fool of a girl."

As soon as she heard those words, Fiona spun around and watched her mother very carefully.

Margaret McCabe was not one to stand by and allow anyone to badmouth her daughter, even though she was a dab hand at criticising Kate herself, mainly for the same reasons as Fiona did. Client or no client, it was immediately clear that Margaret wasn't about to make an exception for this woman.

"And who," she said icily. "May I ask are you? Do you think you can come in here and speak to my daughter like that?"

The woman looked taken aback.

"Well? Cat got your tongue?"

"No, I..." she clasped a hand to her chest and looked so astonished that Fi was on the verge of hurrying forward to catch her if she keeled over.

Oh no, was all she could think. Not again. Ballycashel had had two suspicious deaths that year, and she'd been thrown into the middle of those investigations. She did *not* want to make it a hat trick, not for all the money in the world.

Luckily, though, it appeared Mrs Flanagan was just being dramatic. She didn't fall. Nor did she give any sign of relenting and going away. She cleared her throat and looked around at them with a withering expression that would have curdled milk.

"I am here," she announced. "Because I am not at all confident that you have the capacity to cater an event of this calibre."

"I assured you I could before you signed the contract. It's for fifty people. Fiona has more than that in the pub on a nightly basis. Isn't that right, Fi?"

Fiona nodded. It wasn't strictly true, but what was she going to do? If she disagreed she'd never hear the end of it.

"I wasn't talking about *numbers*."

"What were you on about so?" Fiona was tired, covered in marinade, and not at all inclined to make nice to this rude woman.

"I was referring to the quality of our guests."

Three blank faces gazed back at her.

"My daughter may be a bit of a hippy, but I can assure you that our guests are not. Her father is a very important man!"

"And a saint as well, for putting up with you," Margaret muttered under her breath.

"Pardon me?"

"Fair play to him, I said."

"A *very* prominent solicitor in Dublin," she went on. "Quite why she felt the need to *rebel* like this I don't know. But I'll have you know I won't stand for a poor quality event. I won't embarrass myself like that, do you hear?"

"Of course, Mrs Flanagan," Kate said. "I understand your concerns, even if there's no reason at all for them. You needn't worry. Do you know, we're catering an event for the daughter of a famous singer in a few days. Isn't that something? He was very big in the showband era."

Mrs Flanagan eyed her suspiciously. "Was he now?"

"Yes, he was quite something. At one stage he took top billing in every hall around the country. So you can relax. If someone of that standing is comfortable with our venue, your guests will be."

"Who is he?"

"The singer?"

"Of course the singer. Who else did you think I was talking about?"

Kate faltered for a moment, but it was only obvious to those in the room who were related to her by blood. "I can't tell you that. I signed a confidentiality agreement."

"What? You can't have. You didn't sign one with us."

"I didn't need to."

"What? Don't you know my husband is one of the top solicitors in this country?"

"Oh believe me, I know it well. But he's not

exactly a *celebrity*. I wish I could tell you but my hands are tied."

Mrs Flanagan blinked and looked around at them. Fi and her mother both nodded.

"That's all well and good, but how am I to know he's a man of taste? I want to come and see the function."

"You want to see it?" Kate wheezed.

"Yes."

Kate shook her head. "No. I can't just let a random stranger—"

"I've paid a lot of money for this. If you were a proper venue you'd let future clients see what kind of an event you can put on. You said it was in a few days."

Kate sighed as if someone had let the air out of her. "Wednesday."

She turned and swanned out of the restaurant, leaving three stunned women standing in her wake.

"Oh my God, Kate," Fiona hissed when she'd gone over and closed the door. "What have you just done?"

Kate shook her head. "I don't know. I was improvising."

"Why did you tell her she could come?"

"Because she wouldn't have taken no for an

answer. You've seen what she's like. She's entitled to see an event I organised. I think I offered most of my potential brides that option."

Fiona rolled her eyes. "That's not the same, you know."

"Ah but sure what if she remembers? I can't go back on promises I've already made."

"You can't, no, but why would you go promising her a thing like that? What are you going to do when she turns up looking for a famous face?"

Kate shook her head. "I'll point him out."

"What do you mean you'll point him out?"

"Exactly what I said!"

"But he's not famous."

"Yes he is."

"What would you know? You weren't even born."

"Neither were you."

"Mrs Kilcomer told me. She said it was well before my time but her husband used to be very well known."

"Yeah right!"

"It's true!"

"Mam, tell her it's not. If he was a famous singer you'd know him. You were into the showbands weren't you?"

Margaret McCabe nodded. "What did he say his name was?"

"Kilcomer."

"Doesn't ring a bell."

Fiona frowned at her sister. "See? You know Mam knows all the singers from that era. God knows we had to listen to the tapes enough when we were growing up."

"What are you saying then?"

She shrugged. "That he's feeding you a pack of lies."

"Why would he do that though?"

"No idea."

Kate rolled her eyes. "You're so dramatic Fiona. Give it a rest and help me chop these, would you?"

Fi was about to object, but she bit her tongue. It was already going to be a long night without her starting an argument she didn't need to start. And wasn't Kate right? Why on earth would she think a man she'd never met was lying?

3

The next day was hectic, but it was surprisingly manageable. The McCabes turned out in force. Enda had been signed up to take the wedding photographs. Marty was enlisted to hire a vintage car and drive the bride and her father from their hotel on the outskirts of town to the church and deliver the newlyweds to the reception afterwards. Ben made a smart-looking (if reluctant) waiter, helping Fi and Granny Coyle. Mrs McCabe oversaw things in the kitchen, and Francis was in his element acting as MC for the proceedings once the party reached the pub.

There were a few little snags, but nothing Kate couldn't talk her way out of.

Now that Fi was on good terms with her neighbour Mrs Davis, they were able to relax a little knowing there'd be no calls to the Gardaí. Not that that was any guarantee the sergeant wouldn't come around to cause trouble. Fiona wasn't exactly on good terms with him.

But he hadn't appeared and they spent a productive—if exhausting—two hours working together to get everything cleaned so they had a clean slate to work with the next day.

They finally got home at four in the morning, and everyone headed straight for the kitchen table. They'd taken turns to eat after the guests had been served, but that felt like a very long time ago. Mrs McCabe heated a frozen lasagne and they all sat around the table heaving into the food.

"And we get to do it all again in two days," Kate said brightly.

Marty dropped his plate heavily on the table, causing them all to jump—they were so tired that their nerves were jagged and the unexpected noise didn't exactly help matters.

"You're joking, right?"

Kate looked at him as if he was mad. "No, of course not."

"You mean there's another wedding on *Wednesday*? I take it they don't need the car?"

"Well not that car in particular," she said, taking

a huge forkful of lasagne. "They've asked for a VW Beetle."

"Kate for God's sake! Do you know the hassle Davey put me through when I wanted to hire the Morris Minor from him at short notice? Why can't you tell me these things in advance?"

"I've been incredibly busy, Marty."

"So have I. I've been running the hardware shop. As far as I knew, you've been sitting around ever since you quit your job at the hairdressers."

"I haven't quit. I just reduced my hours so I could focus on my business plan."

"And drinking all my coffee," Fiona muttered. She didn't particularly care. She'd stopped opening the bar up in the mornings, so somebody had to help her work her way through her supply of coffee beans. "What are you doing anyway? It's weird to see you without your head stuck in your phone."

Kate snapped her notebook shut and looked at Marty and Fi in turn, eyes narrowed. "Working out my numbers."

"Shouldn't you have done that *before* you agreed to plan those weddings?"

"Do you want to keep talking or do you want to get paid?"

Enda grinned. "I thought we were donating our

skills, like the last time I cancelled a paying client to help out my dear little sister."

"Yeah, I mean there's no way I'd have worked for you if you weren't my sister."

Their father laughed. "Ben, I'm quite frankly amazed that *anyone* managed to get you to work for them. Good on you, love. If this wedding thing falls apart, you can always go get a job in the dole office. I'm sure they'd be dying to get their hands on someone like you."

It was Mr McCabe's turn to receive one of Kate's filthy looks. "So that's it? You all think this was some silly novelty idea where I lost money, but sure it's grand anyway cause wasn't I doing *something*?"

None of them would meet her eyes.

"So you're not expecting to get paid?"

Fiona snorted. "Let's just put it this way—if you weren't my sister, there's no way I would have put in all that work for the sake of backache and zero money."

Kate pulled her notebook closer to her and smiled enigmatically. "That's great so."

The others looked at each other.

Marty lunged for the notebook. He was leaning back in his chair looking at it before Kate had even realised it was missing.

"That's mine! Give it back! It's an integral part of my business!"

"Integral part of your business. Would you listen to her! Been watching too much Dragon's Den I'd say."

"Shut up, Enda! Marty, give me back my book."

He didn't. He flicked through the pages to the last entry. They all watched in silence as his eyes skimmed the page.

"Good God Kate," he muttered.

"What? What's she gone and done?" Fi asked, snatching the book from him.

Fiona found the page he'd been looking at and steeled herself. Had Kate borrowed money from their parents and lost it on the first wedding? And what were they going to do now that there were three more coming up, including one in two days' time? They'd have no choice but to cancel. It was the right thing to do, but Fi couldn't stand the thought of letting three brides down so close to their weddings. She shuddered. Especially not if it meant dealing with an angry Mrs Flanagan.

Then she realised what she was looking at.

It was a profit and loss statement of sorts. It looked nothing like the ones she'd studied in college, but that was what it was.

She looked up at Kate.

"Does this list all of your expenses aside from our time?"

"No. It's got everything in there. There's a line for contractors."

Fi's eyes widened even more. "You mean you've factored in paying us for our time?"

"Well you just said you didn't want to be paid, so I'll have to change it."

"No, I said I didn't *expect* you to pay us. Two different things."

Kate shook her head.

Fi didn't see the sense in quibbling. She was too astonished to argue with Kate, which she could do later once she'd recovered from the shock of what she'd just seen.

"Kate, it says here that you've made a profit. Is that right? You're sure these numbers stack up?"

"Yeah," Kate said defensively. "I may not have done business in college, but I know how to add and subtract."

"What is it?" Francis said sharply, pushing his plate away. "What's she gone and done?"

Fiona shook her head. She'd double and triple checked at this stage, and there was no denying it.

"She's gone and turned a profit, Dad. And a

pretty significant one at that. Are you seriously telling me these numbers are right?"

Kate nodded. "Yup. So I take it I can count on your support for the next wedding on Wednesday?"

"You sound just like a politician," Enda groaned.

"Is that a yes or a no?"

Fiona threw the book to him and waited until he saw the figure Kate had included for photographer fees.

Sure enough, a few moments later his face lit up and he nodded. "Definitely. Absolutely."

4

Attitudes in the McCabe family were vastly different early on the morning of the second wedding. No one was haranguing Kate for dossing on her phone when everyone else was working. In fact, Mrs McCabe had spoken to them all privately to tell them to leave her alone.

Kate had some sort of magic touch when it came to making money. And as reluctant as Fi was to admit it, she hadn't exactly inherited the same skill. She was set to earn more from these weddings than she'd taken in at the bar over the past several months.

"Just think what I could do if I had a purpose-built venue for weddings and other events. I mean, I could go to the hotel, but all the profits are going to be sucked up by their hire fees and they won't let you use outside catering."

"I haven't told you my hire fees yet," Fi said, carefully placing a vase in the middle of the table they were working on. "They've just gone up."

They'd pulled all the chairs and tables out of the bar for the second wedding. Kate had sourced large round tables and Chiavari chairs from a hire company. The chairs were plastic, but they looked surprisingly realistic with their satin-sheen gold bodies and red velvets seats.

"I'm sure you'll give me family rates. It's only fair."

Fi frowned suspiciously. "Yeah. You don't seem to be pushing as hard as I might expect on this."

"Why would I?" Kate flicked her hair back and scribbled something on the clipboard she was carrying. "Even counting your fees I'm still making a lot of money out of this."

I should have charged her for using the bar as her office, Fi thought, shaking her head. At the back of it all, she was proud of her younger sister's savvy, even if this event would be trickier than the last.

"This is really fancy," she remarked when they had the first full table completed.

It wasn't just the chairs. They'd dressed the table with a flimsy voile cloth and little confetti stars. Kate had hired silver candelabras and red candles to go in the centre of each of the five tables. Surprisingly for tables of their size, they fit into the back area of the pub with room to spare. Marty and Colm would clear them out to the back after the meal and store them on their sides with the legs folded back so that the area could be used as a dance floor later.

Fi stood back and admired their handiwork. The bar looked nothing like it usually did. It struck her as strange, and not for the first time.

"Why didn't they go to a hotel?" she asked suddenly.

"Because I gave them a better deal," Kate shot back straight away.

Fi shook her head. "No; I mean I'm sure you did, but it seems strange. We talked about it. We could see the appeal of getting married in a traditional pub. But this? It looks more like a standard wedding at a luxury hotel."

"If you say so."

"I do. I've been to five weddings already this year, and it reminds me of something at a big hotel for three hundred guests. No expense spared."

Kate smiled. "They certainly haven't spared any expense, I can tell you that."

"Why then? Usually weddings this fancy have hundreds upon hundreds of guests. It's all about seeing and being seen. Do you not think it's weird that there are only fifty of them?"

"No. I don't think we could fit three hundred people in the pub."

"That's not what I meant. It's weird that they want all this opulence and they didn't go for a venue that'd hold more people and offer this kind of stuff as standard."

Kate shrugged. "I don't know. I'm just counting the money this one is bringing in. I can't believe it, Fi."

"Neither can I."

"Hey, come on you two," Margaret McCabe called. "Get a move on. The clock is ticking."

———

THE PUB LOOKED like something out of a fairy-tale when Fi and her family were finished setting up. They were ready with an hour to spare. This time, Kate had hired Mrs Davis to help out with serving the food and two men to work at the bar. The bride's family wanted enough staff on hand to ensure none of their guests needed to wait for anything. Kate had willingly complied and charged them through the nose for it. She had hired them black and white uniforms this time, unlike the first wedding where they had worn black t-shirts and jeans.

The first guest to arrive wasn't a guest, as such. It was Mrs Flanagan and her daughter, who looked almost apologetic to be there. Indeed, she pulled Fiona aside the first opportunity she got.

"I'm sorry about my mother."

"Don't be. Mothers go a little crazy around weddings."

"Are you married?"

"God no. I can't imagine what my mother would be like. She's over there. See for yourself."

Margaret was fussing over a floral arrangement at the other side of the room.

"Ah, yeah. I see what you mean."

Kate came hurrying over with her arms out. "Marie! Mrs Flanagan! What a pleasure to see you!"

Marie hugged Kate, while her mother hung back and stared at the McCabe sisters with barely disguised loathing.

"Okay, we're expecting the first guests in about forty-five minutes, so feel free to take a look around the room now. Obviously it's different to the setup you wanted, Marie, but it's good to see it all set up for an event like this. I've to run off back to the church now. Can I just ask that you return to the snug when the guests arrive? With a small tight-knit affair like this, it's more difficult to have onlookers present than if we were at a hotel, say."

"Of course," Marie said with a smile at the exact moment that her mother tossed her head and muttered, "if I'd had my way, we'd have booked a hotel."

They ignored her—there was too much to do for Fi and Kate to pay much attention to their difficult client.

Fi hurried behind the bar and checked the display of champagne flutes and wine glasses. She shook her head, smiling at the Guinness tap that had been reinstalled for the occasion. She had to hand it to Kate; she was quite business-focused and persuasive when she put her mind to it. The groom had requested draught beer and Kate had organised it herself. Fi made a mental note to remove the temporary tap just as soon as the wedding was over.

She'd never hear the end of it if Gerry Reynolds walked in and saw it there. He was having a lot of trouble accepting the fact that she'd restyled the pub as a cocktail bar and as such wasn't offering draught beers anymore.

Once she was assured that the bar setup was going to plan, she bustled back to check on the tables.

IN NO TIME at all it was almost one. Fi hurried to the bar just as the bell above the outer door rang.

"Right," she hissed to Jason, one of the barmen they'd hired for the day. "All ready?"

He nodded. He was a lucky find. He was from Cloher, a town nearby. Fi hadn't known him before Kate announced she'd hired him to work the bar. He was an eager young guy, far more likeable than Tom, the other barman Kate had found, who was a Ballycashel local who'd always kept to himself.

"Yup, all good to go," Jason said confidently, straightening his bow-tie.

"Great. I'll take a tray of drinks and give them out at the door."

She walked out from behind the bar and hurried

over to Angus, who was on door duty, greeting the guests.

It was a far fancier event than the first wedding, for two reasons. One, the bride had opted for a much more extravagant package than the first bride had— Kate had tapped the side of her nose and whispered something about money being no object (it was another reason why Fi wondered about the choice of a pub for the venue, but she'd said nothing, preferring to think about her hire fee). The second reason was the presence of Mrs Flanagan. Annoying or not, she was still spending a lot of money on her daughter's wedding. Kate had added some subtle enhancements at the last minute in order to reassure her difficult client that there'd be nothing shabby about her daughter's wedding, even if it was to be held in a pub.

Soon the bar was thrumming with activity. The soothing sounds of harp music were a far cry from Fiona's usual playlist, but she couldn't help but relax at the sound. The harpist was a friend of Marty's who used to play in the pub when her parents had run it. She was a gifted musician.

Everything was going well, she was pleased to see. They had about thirty-five or forty guests present. The newlyweds and their immediate families were still back at the churchyard having some photos taken, according to Kate's text.

Reassured that there were no disasters to resolve, Fiona refilled her silver tray with champagne flutes and weaved amongst the guests. Right on cue, Mrs Davis emerged from the kitchen behind of the bar with a tray of canapés they had been up at the crack of dawn to make.

It was a joy to see the pub so full of lively, happy people. She smiled as she approached Marie and Mrs Flanagan and subtly offered them a glass of champagne each.

Even the difficult woman looked content—a far cry from how she'd come across just days before. She was sitting in the snug—out of harm's way and behaving herself.

Amazingly, Fiona found she was more relaxed than she had been in a long time.

The door opened. She glanced back and saw Angus gesturing madly.

The bride and groom were about to arrive. They had opted for a different format to most Irish weddings where the bride and groom make a dramatic entrance when all the guests are seated for dinner. This bride and groom weren't interested in spending all day having their photographs taken. They wanted to spend time with their guests.

Fiona hurried to the bar and refilled her tray. By the time the bridal party were entering the bar, she was standing by the door opposite Angus, with a tray full of drinks in her hands.

She smiled over at him. They were taking things slowly and had been on several dates over the past few months, but despite that caution, she couldn't deny how happy he made her feel. Indeed, she put her enthusiasm for the whole wedding business down to him—even just the year before, she would have taken an ice bath before willingly subjecting herself to a stranger's wedding.

"Welcome to McCabe's," she smiled, holding out her tray. "Congratulations to you both!"

They all took a drink from the tray, except for the bride's father, who took a Guinness from Tom's tray. Fi snuck a glance at her mother as he passed to see if any recognition passed over her face. Margaret's expression didn't change a bit.

Curious, Fiona thought. But then again, the man might have indulged a lot through the years and changed entirely since his heyday back in the sixties and seventies.

There was a cheer as the music stopped and Francis took over the microphone.

"Ladies and gentleman," he intoned in a voice that was remarkably smooth, "please raise your glasses to the bride and groom, Mr And Mrs Hannify."

Fiona was walking back to the bar to drop her tray when this was going on, so she wasn't really looking at what was happening. So when there was a terrifying shriek, it shocked her enough that the five remaining glasses tipped over and fell all over the bar and the counter behind.

She gasped in shock, momentarily forgetting what had caused her clumsiness. It seemed most of the guests had been distracted by the sound of glass breaking and forgotten the scream. Fiona remembered it a moment later with a jolt. She stopped picking up bits of broken glass and turned around, scanning the room.

All she could see were dozens of confused-looking guests, most of them staring in her direction. She was as confused as any of them. Who had screamed like that? It certainly hadn't been interference on the microphone.

When her eyes found the snug it became clear. It

was out of sight to most of the guests who had passed it, but Fiona could see it clearly from the bar.

She wasn't sure which of them had screamed, but it was apparent that the noise had come from one of the Flanagans.

Marie Flanagan was leaning over her mother, who was lying face down on the table, with her empty champagne flute tipped over in front of her.

And her face was as white as a sheet.

5

"Oh my God," Fiona muttered, before quickly remembering herself.

It wasn't a good idea to panic their guests. She had no idea what kind of a stampede it might cause and she didn't want to run the bride's big day.

She hurried towards the snug, finding Kate in the crowd and shooting her the kind of look that could only mean one thing.

Trouble.

At first Kate looked put out, like she had enough to be dealing with, but her expression soon changed. She reached the snug just a few seconds after Fiona.

"Mammy!" Marie Flanagan was wailing. "Mammy! Somebody help her!"

Fiona leaped forward and shuffled around the bench seat until she reached the two women. She shot a quizzical look back at her younger sister, who shook her head.

"Nobody seems to have noticed," she said absently. "I guess that's the one good thing about this mess."

"Would you shut up and help!" Fiona hissed, turning her attention to the Flanagans.

Marie had let out a great sob when she heard Kate's cruel words.

"Please ignore her," Fi said gently. "My sister's a great wedding planner, but I've always suspected she's a bit of a psychopath. Now tell me what happened."

She loosened the woman's collar and held two fingers gently at the base of her neck.

Marie didn't say a word, she just stared at Fi's hands looking utterly stupefied.

"Is she... you know?"

Fi bit her lip and focussed. It was hard to know if what she was feeling was her own frantic pulse or that of Mrs Flanagan.

And then she felt the faintest push against her fingers that was markedly different from her own rapid pulse. And again.

"She's alive," Fiona said, hissing out a breath as she did so. "I've got a pulse."

Kate was still standing at the entrance to the snug, blocking them from the view of any of the guests who happened to walk past to the bar. Thankfully they were all too focused on the stage to pay any attention to what was going on behind them.

"Come on. Do something useful. Call the doctor."

Kate looked even more aghast, but this time at least she had the sense not to say anything.

"What happened, Marie?" Fiona asked gently after they'd eased Mrs Flanagan into a more comfortable position.

The young woman was still beside herself with worry. It was hard to make out what she was saying. Her bottom lip was almost white from her biting down so hard on it. Fiona had to ask her to repeat herself twice before she seemed to come around.

"I don't know. She was fine one minute. Well, her usual self of course, talking about how our guests would think we were paupers having the reception in a place like this. No offence, of course. And then all those people came in. Maybe it was the noise? I don't know." She tucked her hair behind her ears. "All of a sudden she just face-planted into the table. Oh God, is she injured? She doesn't look it."

At this, Mrs Flanagan began to stir and Fiona

instinctively moved away from her before forcing herself to get closer again. This was her bar; her responsibility to make sure her guests were okay.

"It's okay, Mammy," Marie crooned. "It's okay. I think you just fainted there."

"Uh?"

"You fainted."

"Uh. Hm."

Marie looked panic-stricken. "Is this normal? After somebody faints?"

Fi shook her head and glanced over at the bar, where Kate was still speaking on the phone. What was taking her so long? "I don't know. I'm sorry. But my sister is calling for help. There are two doctors based here in town so it shouldn't take too long."

It didn't, thankfully. Her father's friend Finbarr burst through the door when Kate was still chatting on the phone.

Fiona got up and hurried to meet him, amazed at how the party was still going on outside of the snug.

"Thanks for coming so quickly."

Finbarr smiled. "Anything for Francis's girls. Where is she?"

He eased his big frame into the snug and set about examining Mrs Flanagan. Fi waited anxiously outside, glancing back at Kate every so often to try and figure out who on earth she was speaking to. It was a miracle she could even hear the other person what with all the noise in the bar.

"Is there anywhere quieter we can bring her?" Finbarr called.

Fiona looked around. The bar was pretty much off-limits in terms of quiet space, and every inch of storage room was now full of supplies for the next two weddings. There was nothing else for it.

"There's my flat upstairs. Do you think she can manage?"

"She'll have to if that's our only option. You lead the way and I'll carry her up—if that's acceptable to you of course?"

The woman muttered something that sounded like 'yes'. As unpleasant as she was, Fiona was heartened to see her recover her bearings somewhat, though she was anxious about her recovering too much and seeing the state of Fiona's flat. They'd been so busy planning the weddings that she hadn't had a chance to clean up for what felt like weeks and could possibly have been months.

She turned around and led Finbarr through the crowd. It was tight in places as people had shoved their chairs right out into the spaces that had been left for servers and guests to move through. Thankfully the guests hadn't been seated yet for the meal, so they were able to make their way through without too much difficulty.

"We're almost there," Fi whispered, as they passed the little makeshift stage where her father was still holding court. He was doing a good job, if the rapt expressions of the guests were anything to go by. The bride and her party were right at the front, she saw to her relief, so they probably hadn't heard anything of the disturbance.

Just as she began to feel as if everything was resolved, there was a bloodcurdling moan from behind her. Fiona spun around in alarm and saw to her horror that the noise had come from Mrs Flanagan. She hurried back, thinking at first that the woman had had another turn.

But she hadn't.

No, it appeared as if she was trying to say something, but she couldn't get the words out. She had raised a shaking, well-manicured hand. Fi turned and looked where it was aimed.

Mrs Flanagan was pointing straight at the father of the bride.

And she did not look in the least bit star-struck by his presence.

6

By the time they'd reached the top of the stairs, Mrs Flanagan was well enough to deride her current surroundings, though she still wasn't up to using words with more than one syllable.

"Mam, shh. They're helping you. You can't say things like that."

Mrs Flanagan let out a grunt that implied she would say exactly what she felt like saying, thank you very much.

Fi rolled her eyes. She'd had enough experiences of her own with an overbearing mother to be able to see the funny side of it all.

A thought struck her just as the doctor had laid the woman gently on Fi's bed, which she'd mercifully remembered to tidy that morning.

"Mrs Flanagan, did you recognise Mr Kilcomer after all?"

The woman stared back at her, unmoving like a stone.

"Remember, we spoke about him. The singer. The father of the bride."

At this, the woman's face fell again and she turned to her daughter looking pale and queasy. "Liar!"

"Calm down, Mam. It's okay! What's wrong? Didn't you like his music or something?"

Marie turned to Fi. "She's very particular about her music. I suppose she might have known him after all and just not been a fan of his work."

Fi shrugged. She'd been curious, but not curious enough to cause a scene and distress the woman any more. "I'd better get back to the wedding down-stairs," she said. "Let us know if there's anything you need."

The doctor nodded gravely. "Yes, please do. I'd like your mother to stay here for at least an hour. I'll be back to check on her."

"What is it, doctor? What's wrong with her?"

"Nothing more than a fainting spell," he said calmly. "Happens to people all over the country every day. All the same, I'd like to check on her in an hour to make sure she's returned to normal. I'll be back then. If you think she's back to normal before then, here's my card. Give me a call if she recovers sooner."

"YOU'RE VERY DEDICATED," Fiona observed as she closed the door behind them and left the Flanagans alone in her bedroom. She wasn't terribly keen on the idea, but what else was she going to do? They'd soon be asking the guests downstairs to take their seats for the meal and there was nowhere else to put Mrs Flanagan. She couldn't very well ask an ill woman to leave the premises, could she?

Finbarr laughed and shook his head. "I was on the way to the golf course when your sister rang me. I'll be very dedicated indeed so long as it helps me make my tee time."

Fi grinned. Finbarr had been obsessed with golf for as long as she could remember, though he'd never managed to convince her father to join him in that passion. Francis McCabe was staunchly anti-golf, mainly because he considered it unIrish in the extreme.

Fi wasn't really fussed either way—golf was just

something she'd never really given much thought to before. Until recently.

She had reason to believe that there was something fishy going on between the local Garda sergeant and a prominent member of the golf club. She and her grandmother had been sniffing around trying to get to the bottom of it, but the trail had run frustratingly cold.

Still, that didn't stop her wanting to get to the bottom of whatever was going on.

"Who are you golfing with?"

"Dr Grimes."

"Ah," she said, wishing she didn't feel so disappointed. Sergeant Brennan was a berk of the highest order, but even he wasn't foolish enough to be a visible presence at the place where he conducted his dodgy dealings. She cleared her throat. "Do you ever see Sergeant Brennan around the club?"

He glanced at her. "Can't say I have. Why? I thought you couldn't stand the man."

She frowned. That was true, of course, but she wondered how her father's friend had come to know it. Her father was a lot of things, but he certainly wasn't a gossip.

Finbarr smiled as if he had read her mind. "Your mother. We had your parents over for dinner not so long ago. She was lamenting the fact that you haven't settled down yet."

"But Mam hates him!" Fi gasped as they reached the bottom of the stairs and she moved forward to open the door that led into the bar. "She hates him more than anyone. How could she say something like that about him after what he did to her? Maybe you took her up wrong. She's not exactly clear at times."

He shook his head. "No," he said in a whisper, because they were in the middle of the party now and the guests had grown quiet as they moved to take their seats at their assigned tables. "I'm sure of it. She mentioned how much she can't stand him, you see."

"Well then she hardly wants me to go out with him so."

Finbarr's eyes twinkled. "The way she put it was she'd try her best to come around to the man if he'd finally catch Fiona's eye and make an honest woman out of her because things don't seem to be moving as fast with this Angus fella as she'd like."

Fiona showed him to the door, forcing herself to hold back the torrent of things she would have liked to have said about her mother. It wasn't exactly a surprise to her, but even so. Was Margaret really that eager to fob her off on whatever nasty piece of work would agree to take her?

She caught sight of Angus, who was now back helping out behind the bar. She shook her head in disbelief. And people had wondered why she was taking things so slowly with him? How could she do anything else the way her mother went on? It was as if Margaret's obsession with her settling down had turned her completely against the idea.

7

Fiona soon forgot her indignation. She was forced to. Even though they'd brought in extra staff and planned the service to the finest details, of course things went wrong.

The bride and groom had chosen two different starters: a salad and a duck terrine. Fiona and her mother had prepared roughly equal quantities of each. They hadn't banked on the majority of guests asking for the vegetarian option.

"We should have known, I'm sorry," Fi simpered to a petite woman in a cerise pink dress and extravagant hat. "Usually we wouldn't have that many vegetarians in, but I suppose it's going to be different for a showbiz crowd."

The woman snapped her head back. "A what?"

"You know," Fi said helplessly, gesturing at the top table. "Showbiz."

The woman still looked confused and Fi wished she hadn't said anything. Had panic made her indiscreet? No, she decided, it was probably just a relative on the groom's side who'd flown in from somewhere and hadn't yet been treated to the tale of the bride's father's fifteen minutes of fame. The idea that he'd insisted on a confidentiality agreement now seemed absurd.

Fiona hurried to the kitchen, idly wondering if the bride's father would take to the stage to sing at any point. Judging from the reaction of Mrs Flanagan, she kind of hoped he wouldn't. She supposed it was possible that the bride, being a proud daughter, must have exaggerated her father's achievements far beyond what they really were.

As soon as they got more salad plated and sent out, there was a frantic scramble to prepare an equivalent number of vegetarian main courses. They'd prepared far more food than was needed for the guests because they'd need staff meals for afterwards, but they still had nowhere near enough vegetable parcels. Mrs McCabe was red-faced and barely coherent by the time she'd prepped an extra twenty parcels and fired them in the oven. At that point, the starter dishes were already being cleared away. Fiona found herself wishing that it was traditional to have speeches between the starter and main courses instead of after dessert was served.

But they did it. When all their guests had been served their main courses and their wine glasses were topped up, Fiona found that she was almost giddy with the sense of achievement that they'd managed to overcome their oversight and saved the day. She even grinned when Kate entered the room, despite all the drama originating with the fact that Kate hadn't thought to ask her bride how many vegetarians were attending.

Right then, though, she could have cared less about the excess meat sitting in the fridge. That was Kate's problem. Besides, she knew it would keep long enough for her to sell them as a dinner special in the pub the following day—not that they didn't have enough to do already.

"It feels good, right?" Kate said, beaming at her as if she'd done Fiona a solid by embroiling her in the whole mess.

Even that couldn't diminish Fi's good humour. "It does. It really does." The sisters left the kitchen and moved out to the bar. There'd be no celebratory champagnes for them just yet, but after all that frantic activity even an ice-cold orange juice was a real treat.

They leaned against the bar staring at each other, too exhausted to think of much to say.

"Have you checked on Mrs Flanagan?"

"God no. I haven't had time."

"She's probably upstairs rummaging through your stuff."

Fiona shrugged. One of the benefits of having an extremely nosy family was that nothing was sacred anymore. "So? If she finds anything interesting I'll be extremely surprised."

Kate laughed. "Oh my God, you have no idea how much I nearly freaked out when I saw the look on your face and then saw her collapsed in the snug."

"I know, right?" She shook her head, giddy from the sudden rush of sugar into her dehydrated body. "I'm so relieved. For a moment I thought we had another murder on our hands."

She froze then, the smile wiped off her face. She looked around with the strangest sinking feeling that she'd jinxed herself.

But no, all of their guests were happily eating and chatting. None of them looked unhappy or outraged. They'd had no complaints. And no murders. Everyone was happy.

Fiona shivered and told herself to relax. The stress of the day was obviously just getting to her, that was all.

"Right," she said, reluctantly pushing away from the bar and standing up straight.

The guests were still some way off from finishing their meals, but that didn't mean there weren't numerous other jobs for them to do. She moved away, standing on the edge of the crowd and looking around to see how many were finished. Her plan was to tidy the kitchen for around ten minutes and then give the go-ahead to the servers to remove the empty plates.

That was her plan. She forgot all about it when her eyes landed on Mrs Davis, standing at the other side of the room. The usually pleasant woman was standing stock still, staring off into the distance.

No, Fiona realised. That wasn't quite right. Mrs Davis was staring at a very definite point in the room. At the top table in fact. It mightn't normally have been worth commenting on, but this wasn't some wistful young woman staring at the bride-to-be and wondering when she'd get her chance. No, there was nothing wistful about Mrs Davis's expression. Her eyes were narrowed and her lips were pursed in distaste. She looked like she was a million miles away from that small town pub in the middle of Ireland.

What's going on with you? Fiona wondered. Mrs Davis had seemed a bit sour until she'd been involved in the last case Fiona and her grandmother had worked to solve. Ever since then, she'd been as sweet and cheery as you could imagine.

She didn't look that way now.

Then Fi rolled her eyes and laughed to herself. It was probably just the way the woman's face was when she was standing alone not talking to anyone. Resting Bitch Face. Fiona was no stranger to the condition. After all, she had endured a lifetime of people telling her to smile, asking what was wrong with her and telling her to cheer up.

She realised belatedly that she'd just wasted five precious minutes judging one of her friends when she should have been using that time more productively. She hurried back to the kitchen to warn the kitchen team that they were about to clear the dinner plates and to be ready to go with the desserts. The sink and draining board were already piled with dirty plates. And that was just from the starters! It would take a long time to clear them all through the pub's little dishwasher, but that couldn't be helped. She didn't know anyone in town with a more advanced system and she wasn't going to go asking at the hotel. After all, they were the town's main wedding venue and therefore the competition.

"We're ready. Go on. Help them clear the plates," Margaret said, sounding calm and cool for a woman in charge of plating fifty desserts.

And again, everything went swimmingly. There was a roughly fifty-fifty split between those wanting profiteroles and those wanting lemon soufflé, meaning they'd catered almost exactly to the crowd and they'd have ten of each left to spare. Fi wasn't worried about that, not when she came from a family of nine, eight of whom lived in the town and had hopelessly sweet teeth.

Once the desserts were served, Fi ran around dividing the servers up so half circulated with teapots and coffee pots, and the other half went around with trays of after dinner drinks for the speeches. It was another aspect of the event that reminded her of larger, more traditional functions, and she again got to thinking about why they'd opted for a pub if they wanted to insist on these traditional little touches.

She didn't mind. Some of those spirits bottles

hadn't even been opened since she reopened the bar. She was happy to use them and charge for them. And Kate had come up with an eye-wateringly expensive price list that for some reason the Kilcomers had agreed to pay.

She smiled to herself. As annoying as her sister was sometimes, she'd had a stroke of genius when she decided to set herself up as a wedding planner. There was no doubt about that.

"Fiona," her mother called, disturbing her from her thoughts. "We need more coffee. Can you make some?"

"Sure." She moved out of the kitchen, towards the bar, and that was when she noticed it.

A deathly hush had fallen over the crowd. At first she thought it was because the speeches were about to begin, but that couldn't be right. Not everybody had been served tea or coffee, and her father's voice hadn't come over the microphone asking everyone to be quiet.

Fiona turned around slowly. In her heart, she already knew what was going on, but she told herself it was too crazy.

She couldn't be right.

She looked around the room.

All of the guests were staring in the same direction, back at the top table. They had no reason to. The speeches hadn't started. Some people had contorted around in what must have been a very uncomfortable way.

Fiona took a step forward, needing to see what was happening.

That was when somebody cried out.

"Oh my God! It's Paddy! He's collapsed! Somebody call an ambulance!"

8

Finbarr hadn't yet returned to check on Mrs Flanagan. Fi called him right after Kate called the ambulance. Nobody in the group was medically trained, so it fell to Fiona, as the licence holder, to attend to the man.

Her mouth had gone dry by the time she reached him, but then some sort of damage limitation set in.

"Move back," she ordered the people around him. "Give him some room. Someone move this table."

He was bent over with his head in his dessert. She moved around behind him and put her hand on his neck to test his pulse. She did it without hesitation, assuming he was just another fainter. Strange, given that it wasn't a particularly warm or humid day.

As soon as her fingers brushed his skin, though, she knew. It was just a fraction too cool.

She turned around and found herself looking into the frantic faces of his family. She swallowed her initial urge to call out to see where the ambulance was. There was no sense in frightening people. Her eyes met the bride's and she felt a burst of pity for the young woman. What a thing to happen. She looked away quickly, not wanting to telegraph the truth in her face.

Thankfully, Finbarr arrived a moment later and hurried through the now-silent crowd.

"Ladies and gentlemen." Francis McCabe's voice boomed from the corner. There was no need for a microphone now, nobody was saying anything. "Please make your way to the bar and give the doctor space to move around."

Fiona mouthed a silent thanks in his direction. She had to hand it to her father—he was certainly calm in a crisis.

Something she couldn't say for her younger sister.

Kate was standing beyond the last table, staring in dismay at the unfolding events. She shook her head as Fi approached.

"He's dead, isn't he? I just know it."

"Keep your voice down! Come here, let's go help..." Fi let out a frustrated sigh. Tom was nowhere to be seen and a confused and frustrated group of guests were beginning to queue in front of a clearly stressed Jason. She grabbed her sister's arm and pulled her forward. "Come on. I don't know where Tom is gone, but we need to serve these people. You take easy orders like beers and wines. I'll look after cocktails and mixed drinks if anyone asks you for them."

"Fiona," Kate muttered, as they met at the drinks fridges a few moments later.

"Not now. Just help me out, okay?"

"I need to know, Fi. I need to know what's wrong with him."

Fi stopped what she was doing and looked at her sister. They were facing away from the guests, but that didn't give her any comfort. This was no time for a heart-to-heart.

"The ambulance will be here soon," she said loudly. "Come on. Serve these people."

"But Fi," Kate hissed, refusing to be silenced. "If this is what I think it is, we need to get the guards here. Right now."

"Oh come off it, Kate. There's no need for drama," she muttered. Her racing pulse told her there was every need for drama, but she tried to fight back that feeling.

"Isn't there, Fi? Think about this. We're due to have another wedding here in a little over a week. We need to get the guards here right now, so they can fill out whatever reports they need to fill out. Otherwise this place is going to be a crime scene!"

"Keep your voice down!" Fiona hissed, turning and glancing at the customers who were waiting at the bar behind them. Sure enough, they were all silent, watching the McCabe sisters with undisguised curiosity. "I mean it, Kate. Now's not the time."

The bell above the door rang and an ambulance crew burst into the bar. The crowd parted to let them through.

"We got a call—"

"Back there," Fiona said, pointing towards the back where Finbarr was tending to the man.

She watched them go, not feeling very hopeful. She hadn't been able to get a pulse. Sure enough, the medical technicians slowed their pace as soon as they caught sight of Finbarr and the man. No words needed to be exchanged—they were professionals; they just knew.

Fi turned away, unable to stomach looking at that scene anymore.

"We've got to call them," Kate hissed. "Now. Imagine what would happen if we didn't have the pub back in time for the next wedding? I'd be ruined."

"I would too," Fi muttered, rolling her eyes. It seemed awfully insensitive to be talking about their businesses at a time like this. Foremost on her mind was the possibility that he'd choked on something or had an allergic reaction to some of the food he'd eaten—either scenario would be a damning black mark on her licence.

"Well then you better get moving. You don't have to call Brennan. I know how things are between the two of you. Call Garda Conway. He likes you."

"I'm not calling anyone, Kate. It's not my job. That's something the ambulance crew do, I suppose. I don't know. I've never been in this situation before."

The bell above the door rang. Fiona didn't even bother to look, assuming it was someone else from the ambulance crew. It was only when her sister groaned that she looked up in surprise.

"Looks like you didn't need to do anything," Kate muttered.

Sergeant Brennan had just marched into the pub. He stormed through the crowd without even slowing his pace. She hurried out from behind the bar and blocked his progress before he reached the table where Finbarr and the medics were tending to the man.

"What are you doing here, Sergeant? This is a private function."

"That's nice, Miss McCabe, but you're aware that as the most serious member of the Gardaí in this town it's my duty to investigate any crimes that occur here."

She shook her head. "How on earth did you get here so fast? The man's not even cold."

She had said it as quietly as she could, not wishing to be indiscreet in front of the family. Sergeant Brennan had no such inhibitions.

"Cold? What are you talking about? Do you mean to tell me he's dead?" His words seemed to echo around the quiet pub.

Fi squeezed her eyes closed, ruing the day she'd ever met Sergeant Brennan. Arch-nemesis didn't even begin to describe the enmity she felt towards him and his insufferable smugness. Not even the fact that he'd been photographed in a compromising situation seemed to diminish his sense of superiority as he lorded it around the town as if he owned the place.

"Can you keep your voice down?"

"I can *not*," he said indignantly, as if she'd just suggested he take his clothes off and dance the Macarena. Now there was an unpleasant thought. "And I suggest you don't say such things again. I could arrest you for perverting the course of justice."

She rolled her eyes. "Just for telling you to keep your voice down in the presence of the man's family? Lovely. I thought this was a democracy."

He ignored her and started gesturing to the two Gardaí who had just entered the pub behind him. While he was busy barking orders at Garda Fitzpatrick, Garda Conway wandered over to Fiona.

"I'm sorry about him. I would have warned you only there was no time."

"How did he know?"

"We get reports of any ambulance callouts in the town. We don't usually pay any attention unless foul play is suspected, but you know how he feels about your—"

Conway!" Brennan barked. "Get over here now! This is an active investigation. You two, I want a list of all the people here. Nobody leaves until you've got that. Alright? Now, get to it."

Kate and Fiona watched dumbfounded as the

Gardaí surged forward and began to corral the crowd, notebooks out. The only small consolation was that they left the immediate family alone for the time being.

The sisters looked at each other, not needing to say anything.

This was serious. It had become serious the moment that man collapsed in his dessert, but now it was even worse. Brennan was after any excuse to harass them and shut Fi down. He'd hounded her on previous occasions when a murder victim happened to have a drink in her bar before he was murdered. What on earth was going to happen if foul play was involved and her bar was an actual crime scene?

"I'm sure he's all talk," Kate said, not sounding very convinced.

"A few minutes ago you were suggesting we call him. Now you don't think the death is suspicious?"

Kate looked away. "I don't know, alright? I've never experienced anything like this before. I don't like it, Fi. He's not an old man. He wasn't on the list of allergies or health complaints that his daughter gave me."

That reminded Fi of something she'd long since forgotten. She sighed. As if this wasn't bad enough.

"Mrs Flanagan," she said with a pained expression. "She's still upstairs."

"Oh no," Kate cried, clasping her hands over her mouth. "She's going to freak out if they march in and confront her up there. There's no way she'll allow Marie to go ahead with the wedding if that happens."

"I'll go warn her."

"Brennan'll never let you through."

"I know that," Fiona said, eyes flashing with mischief. "But they haven't thought to secure the back door, have they. Cover for me."

She turned and hurried towards the front door of the pub, rolling her eyes when she got out unchallenged. It was just like Brennan to sound all self-important and then lead an operation that was so riddled with errors a child might have managed it.

She raced around the corner and hurried along until she reached the side door, which opened right onto the stairs that led up to her flat. She let herself in and hurried up the stairs as quietly as she could, not wishing to alert Brennan to her presence until she'd made the Flanagans a strong cup of tea and explained the situation.

She had it all rehearsed in her head when she got to the flat and unlocked the front door.

Except when she got into her bedroom, she found it was empty.

No Marie. No Mrs Flanagan.

They'd gone.

She stood there confused for a while, before she realised she had better get downstairs before Kate mentioned their upstairs guests to somebody she shouldn't.

9

Fi hurried downstairs, ran around the building and in the front door. She found Kate standing with Brennan, who luckily had his back to her. Fiona was alarmed when she got closer and realised her sister was listing names.

"Mrs Davis."

Brennan turned and scanned the room for the woman, shooting Fiona a contemptuous look as he did so. "Go on."

Kate sighed as if she was only barely holding herself together. "Jason Greene."

Brennan looked around again and frowned. "Who's he? I don't know him."

Kate pointed at the tall man standing beside her mother. "There," she said glumly.

"Is that everyone?"

Kate shook her head. "No. Tom Kenny was also working the bar."

Brennan began his slow scan of the bar again. "Which one is he?"

Kate looked around. A frown slowly came over her face as she turned back to Brennan. "I don't know. I can't see him."

"What do you mean you can't see him?"

She shrugged. "I can't see him. He's not there."

"When did he leave? Did his shift end?"

"No," she said, shaking her head. "He was due to stay on until we closed."

"I see," Brennan said, scribbling something in his notebook. "Is that everyone who was here?"

Kate shot an anxious-looking glance at her sister before she nodded.

"Right," he said solemnly. "I had better examine this table plan."

Fiona darted over to her sister as Brennan stomped off. "What were you doing talking to Brennan?"

Kate blanched. "What was I supposed to do? He started asking me questions. What's the big deal?"

"You know what the big deal is."

Kate stared back at her with a look that suggested she didn't.

"The Flanagans."

"What about them?"

"They're gone, Kate."

"What do you mean they're gone?"

"They're gone. They're not in the flat anymore."

Kate considered this for a moment and then pulled a face. "So? Maybe they got bored of waiting upstairs in that pokey flat of yours."

"Finbarr told them not to leave until he'd come back to examine her. And he only came back when we called him about Mr Kilcomer."

Kate shrugged. "She's a grown woman."

"Did you tell Brennan she was there?"

"No, of course I didn't! I'm not going to tell tales on my own clients."

Fiona looked around. "That's good, I suppose. Now we don't have to explain to him why they're not there anymore. Come on," she said, gesturing to the kitchen. "I suppose we'd better start the clean-up while the guards are talking to the guests."

They'd ushered all the guests into one corner, and the two guards were managing the line to speak to Sergeant Brennan, who had set up in the snug. If they knew anything about Brennan, they knew he'd relish this position and he'd be there for a while.

They went to the kitchen and began to sort

through the mess. The first task they needed to attend to was the plates and glasses. They'd been provided by a hire firm and they needed to be cleaned and returned before twelve the next day or else the hire company would charge penalty fees.

Fi sighed. There was something immensely satisfying about slowly making progress in a huge pile of dishes to be cleaned.

The door flew open just after they'd deposited the first tray of plates in the dishwasher and lowered the lid. Brennan came thundering into the little room, red-faced.

"What do you think you're doing?"

Fiona looked up at him blankly. "Cleaning. We have to get this stuff back to the hire company by tomorrow."

His eyes narrowed. "Well stop it."

"Why? What's it to you?"

He glared at her. "This is a crime scene. My crime scene. I need you to put those down and refrain from touching anything else. Otherwise I'll—"

Fi rolled her eyes. "Do us for perverting the course of justice? Yeah yeah, we know. Just one thing, Sergeant. This isn't a crime scene. Not officially. That man could have died of natural causes, in which case we should have you done for harassment."

He said nothing. He just smiled. "Well that's where you're wrong. The hospital just called. They believe Mr Kilcomer was poisoned. This is very much a murder investigation. Now, Garda Fitzpatrick will escort you off my crime scene. There's no need for you to be here."

10

To make matters worse, Brennan had decided that the flat upstairs was part of his crime scene too. Fiona was officially banished from her own home and place of business while the guards interviewed the guests. Her family had all been turfed out of there too.

Margaret must have called her mother as soon as she left the bar, because Rose was waiting outside for them when they left the bar after trying in vain to reason with Garda Fitzpatrick.

"Are you alright, love?"

Fiona shook her head, still unable to believe what was going on. "No. Brennan's saying the man was poisoned. I have no idea what's going on. We were right there when it happened!"

Rose had left straight after the desserts were

served, so she had missed all of the chaos. But when Fiona started to tell her what had happened, she held her hand up. "Mrs Davis already told me. I'm on my way round to her now—I thought I'd wait for you two first. Come on."

"But we need to be here for when they finish up! We've got to get that stuff back otherwise the hire company will fine me."

Rose looked sympathetically at her younger granddaughter. "I don't think that's going to happen anytime soon, knowing Brennan. And there's not much sense in us freezing ourselves here. Come on, we'll go over to Mrs Davis."

Fiona narrowed her eyes as she remembered the strange way Mrs Davis had been looking at Paddy Kilcomer. She'd written it off as the woman having a naturally sour face, but now she wasn't so sure.

"Something's bothering you," Rose announced.

Fi shook her head. "No." Not only had she become friends with Mrs Davis, her grandmother had too. And Fiona didn't feel right making such accusations about Rose's friends when she had no proof.

"Spit it out."

"It's nothing."

Rose raised an eyebrow as she wrapped her thick

coat around herself. "Out with it or let's go. I'm cold. I can't deal with it at my age."

"Fine," Fi muttered. "I thought it was nothing at the time, but I saw Mrs Davis glaring at that man. And now he's dead."

"Glaring at him?"

"During the meal. She was just standing there frowning at him."

"Well come on. You can ask her yourself when we go round there."

Fiona baulked. "I'm not going to ask her if she murdered that man."

"Why not? She wears her heart on her sleeve. She'll probably admit it."

Fiona sighed. The cold was starting to get to her too. They had too much to do over the next week and a half without adding the flu into the mix. "Come on. It's probably nothing. Let's go."

Fi and her granny moved, leaving Kate standing on the pavement, staring at her phone.

"Come on, Kate."

Kate shrugged. "Go on without me. I'll just stand here until I freeze. What else can go wrong? My business is ruined before it's even really started."

"Ah come on, Kate. These things happen." Fi stopped. She was still treating this as an unfortunate medical event but it was so much more. She shook her head. "We'll get through it. Of course we will. It's not our fault. You've been paid for the wedding."

Kate rolled her eyes. "It's not this wedding I'm worried about. It's the next one. Nobody wants to get married at a crime scene."

"They won't find out. We won't tell them. It's not relevant."

Kate sighed and started walking. "They already have. I've just got an email from Marie wanting to cancel her wedding."

"Ah I'm sure you can talk her round."

"She sounds pretty adamant to me. Look." Kate thrust the phone in front of Fi's face just as they caught up with their granny outside Mrs Davis's shop. It was laid out similarly to the pub in that there were two doors: the one that led into the shop and one that led to the stairs up to the flat above it.

Fiona read Marie Flanagan's email as they walked up the stairs. Kate was right—she seemed pretty set on cancelling the wedding. Her email was brief and to-the-point.

I would like to invoke the cancellation clause in our contract in light of what happened earlier today.

Kate sighed. "I should never have taken on a

client who had a bigshot solicitor for a father. What was I thinking? This is a mess."

Fi was silent as they reached the top of the stairs and Mrs Davis welcomed them into the flat. It was funny to think that Mrs Davis had been a nuisance neighbour to Fi just a few short months before. Now they were friends. Mrs Davis had grown close to Rose too and the two women now spent most of their nights marauding around Ballycashel tricking other pensioners into betting against them at cards.

On this occasion, though, Fi wasn't particularly happy about seeing her friend.

"My granddaughter thinks you're a murderer," Rose announced before Mrs Davis had even had time to close the door behind them.

"What?"

"You heard me. Tell her, Fiona."

Fiona turned and stared helplessly into Mrs Davis's green eyes. She glanced at Rose, who nodded encouragingly, as if Fiona was about to perform her first song at a school play and not accuse a friend of murder.

She sighed. "I saw you staring at the man who died. Staring like you couldn't stand the sight of him."

Mrs Davis gasped and turned around. "Did you hear that Rose?"

"I did," Rose said firmly. "That's why I told her to ask you straight out. That granddaughter of mine is always stuck in her head with her theories. Did you do it?"

Mrs Davis laughed and shook her head. "You're asking did I murder him?"

"I am," Rose said, clearly relishing this. "Did you?"

"No, of course not," she said, shaking her head and laughing as if it was the funniest thing she'd ever heard. "Good God, Fiona. Not even Brennan thought I did it. He barely asked me anything earlier and you know how that man likes to point the finger. If I was frowning it was because of the headache I got after sneaking those brandies at the bar with you, Rose. You're an awful bad influence." She turned and went to the kitchen, leaving the two McCabe girls staring after her in shock and Rose Coyle doubled over with laughter.

"Ye were sneaking the brandy? I paid for those bottles, Granny."

Fiona couldn't stop herself from laughing at her sister's complete indignation. As soon as she sat down on the sagging velvet couch, though, her good humour evaporated. A man had been murdered in her pub. Her pub that was costing her nothing but time and stress and not offering much in return.

Should she just cut her losses and leave town? She had no doubt that Brennan was going to stall the investigation as much as possible just to keep her business from operating. Maybe he'd even try and accuse her or a member of her family of the murder. Because it wouldn't be the first time he tried something like that.

Kate sat down beside her and stared at her. "What's wrong with you?"

Fiona shook her head. "Have you forgotten already? Someone was murdered in my bar."

"Of course I haven't forgotten. It happened at my event. It was my bride's father."

Fi sighed and shook her head. "It's all so weird. We were there and we saw nothing suspicious."

Kate nodded sadly.

It was only when she played the day back in her head that she got back to thinking about the Flanagans.

"In all the drama of the murder—or the supposed murder—I forgot all about Mrs Flanagan fainting. And it didn't seem important at the time, but do you remember when we passed the wedding party on the way upstairs? Finbarr was carrying her and she was glaring at him. I thought it was because she recognised him after all, but this wasn't the way a superfan might look at a guy she used to idolise."

"How was she looking at him then?"

Fiona sucked in a breath and took a biscuit from the plate Mrs Davis offered. "I don't know. Weirdly. Like she was absolutely disgusted with him or something." She took a bite and chewed it for a while as she tried to get her thoughts straight.

"Oh look, Rose. She's moved on from me and she's accusing somebody else of murder now."

Fiona was about to laugh and deny it, but then she thought of something else. She sat up straight and stared at her sister with wide, bewildered eyes. "Kate, how could Marie possibly know about the murder unless she was there when it happened?"

Kate shook her head slowly. "I don't know. From the paper maybe?"

"No," Fi said. "No, I've been on the news websites since then. There's nothing on there about a murder in Ballycashel. And think about it. The guards only found out themselves not so long ago."

"So...?"

"So Marie is cancelling because of the murder.

But how exactly does she know there was a murder, Kate?"

Mrs Davis chose that moment to interrupt and insist they come into the kitchen for a cup of tea and stop accusing people of murder. Fi was about to say something else, but the older woman beat her to it.

"Listen to me. You'll only drive yourselves mad worrying about this. The guards will do their job and get to the bottom of it."

"But I think we're on to something here?"

Mrs Davis smiled and shared a look with Rose. "Oh yes? Like you thought I was the murderer five minutes ago."

Fiona couldn't think of anything to say to counter that, even though she knew this was different. They moved silently into the kitchen and sat around the table as Mrs Davis doled out pretty china cups and matching saucers.

Something didn't add up no matter how much she tried to tease it out. Marie Flanagan should have had no way of knowing about the murder—unless they were somehow involved in it before they fled Ballycashel.

11

It took another two hours of forced high spirits before Fi could get away from Mrs Davis's house. Her friend had their best interests at heart, of course—that much was obvious—but trying to tell Fi to stop thinking about the murder was like telling her to stop needing air.

Especially now that she'd stumbled upon an anomaly. Had she and Kate somehow facilitated a murder?

It wasn't a simple matter of just going to the guards and telling them about Mrs Flanagan. That would only throw up a whole load of questions—questions she wasn't sure she could answer.

Would they believe her? Or would they think that Kate and Fi's silence about the Flanagans' presence in the flat was an attempt to cover up for something more sinister?

She stopped and turned around, tucking her hair behind her ears. Maybe Mrs Davis was right and she was only driving herself demented over this. She should go back there to the calm, cosy little flat and have another cup of tea and one of Mrs Davis's delicious oatmeal biscuits.

She had only gotten a few metres when she stopped again.

No.

This was just burying her head in the sand and hoping it would all go away.

And it wouldn't, would it? Not if Mrs Flanagan was behind the murder.

That seemed like a plausible scenario to Fiona. The way the woman had reacted to seeing him... Maybe it had been a surprise for her; she hadn't planned it but had been spurred on to act just as soon as she'd recovered her bearings.

Why else would she just vanish before the doctor gave her the all-clear?

But more importantly, how else could her daughter have known about the crime almost at the same time as the Gardaí?

Fi turned around again. Her flat was still off

limits to her, and she'd been heading towards her parents' house.

Now she took a different route; went left instead of turning right for the McCabe's house. Soon she was pushing open the door of Phelan's, one of the other pubs in town.

It was popular with the older crowd and they often had good traditional bands in there, but that didn't interest her right then. No, she was more interested in Phelan's for the fact that it was Garda Stephen Conway's regular haunt.

She opened the door and six grey heads turned to look at her. She realised her mistake there and then. The fact that the regulars at the bar were looking at her with interest was probably down to the fact that word of the murder had spread through the town.

That in turn meant that it probably wasn't a good idea for her to be seen talking to Garda Conway. People would talk. She knew all about the sort of cynical talk that spread like wildfire in a small town like Ballycashel.

"Oh hello there, Fiona," the owner, Jimmy, said as she approached him. As if he hadn't watched her like a hawk when she entered the place.

But she had to play along. If she didn't, who

knew what kinds of rumours they'd start spreading about her.

"Hello there Jimmy," she said cheerily.

"Haven't seen you in these parts lately."

She shrugged. That was part of the game, of course. She couldn't reveal too much straight off the bat like that because they'd see it coming a mile away. No, she had to let them tease the information out of her so they'd feel as if she hadn't really wanted to say anything at all; that they'd tricked it out of her.

Which was a lot of effort when she really just wanted to get over to Garda Conway and find out if the guards had any serious lines of enquiry.

"Ah, sure a change is as good as a holiday."

Jimmy was polishing a glass with a worn and tattered cloth. "I hear you'd a bit of trouble over at that bar of yours."

Fiona could have leapt across the bar and kissed him. Dancing around the subject was a risky business, of course, because if she came across as too coy then they'd all start thinking that she was somehow involved in the murder.

She nodded slowly, trying to keep the relief and gratitude off her face and out of her voice. "Yeah, I'll say. To be honest, all I want to do is pour a big glass of wine and relax after all the mayhem, but of course they're treating the bar as a crime scene so I can't go back there."

"Are they?" one of the men gasped, turning around so fast she was surprised he didn't get whiplash from the force of it.

She nodded, deadpan as possible. "They are, Seanie. It's the strangest thing. And do you know." She looked around at them all as if weighing up whether to share what she knew, when in reality she knew well that all of them knew exactly what was going on over at her bar.

Six pairs of eyes willed her on; willed her to just trust them and hand over another titbit of information. She smiled to herself as she imagined how wound up Kate would be if she knew Fiona was out there gossiping about the murder instead of trying to contain the story and protect the fledgling wedding planning business.

But that was the price she had to pay.

Fiona sighed and shook her head. "I really shouldn't say anything."

"Why, Fiona love? Sure what's there to tell? You're among friends here."

"I know," she said, hoping her expression looked suitably pained. "It's just... it doesn't feel right seeing as it's an active Garda investigation and all that."

No one said a word. Seanie nodded encouragingly, as if she should keep talking and get the whole matter off her chest.

She blinked a few times and glanced away. "It's just awful. Do you know, they think he was murdered?"

"Who?"

"Shhh."

Her audience was clearly at odds about how much they should probe her for information.

Good, she thought. *Drag it out.*

"That man, of course," she said. "The wedding guest."

"Father of the bride is what I heard," Johnnie slurred, immediately receiving a dig in the ribs from Seanie beside him.

Fi widened her eyes as if she couldn't understand how he'd made such a lucky guess. Because while there was no way that news could have made it as far as Dublin in that time, there was every likelihood that everyone in town now knew about it.

"How... I... oh God," she said, burying her face in her hands. "So it's out already? This'll ruin us! I'm not even worried about me and the pub, but my sister's after putting her heart and soul into that wedding planning business."

"Ah no, I'm sure it'll be grand."

The audience was beginning to look uncomfortable. It was easy to see why. The most female emotion a lot of them had experienced in the past twenty years was from TV shows. They just didn't know where to look or how to act.

She felt bad, in a way—they were nice men and she'd known many of them her whole life.

But this was the act she had to put on to find out what she needed to know without creating a whirlwind of gossip.

Finally, after a long and awkward few minutes of trying to make herself cry and failing miserably, Seanie patted her arm. "You'll be grand. What are you worrying about?"

"Nobody's going to use her again," she whispered, shaking her head. "We had no idea. How do you, sure? The man was a singer. Who'd want to murder him? I think it's all a big mistake personally." She sighed dramatically. "The worst thing is the guards aren't telling us anything. That's my business over there and they've pushed me out and more or less said I have to stay away until they tell me I can go back. We have a load of stuff in there that Kate hired. It's costing her a fortune."

That part, on the other hand, involved no acting whatsoever. As of that moment, she'd had no indication from the guards when they might be finished examining the pub. Brennan had just smiled his obnoxious smile and shook his head when she'd asked him for an estimate.

"Ah Fiona."

She swallowed. This was going to seriously damage her standing in the town, but she couldn't see another choice. "Ah Fiona nothing. You don't understand. Here I am, trying to follow in my father's footsteps, and now someone's come along and ruined everything! I might never get back into the pub."

"Ah, lookit," Jimmy muttered, looking around the bar with an expression on his face that said he was utterly disgusted by what he'd heard. He found what he was looking for in the corner. Or rather, he found *who* he was looking for. "Garda, are you hearing this? It's not right. This poor lassie is half out of her mind with worry. And ye not telling her a thing. You must know something."

Fiona held her hands up and shook her head. "No, Jimmy. No, you don't need to do that. I don't..."

She stood as if she planned to leave. Seanie grabbed her arm before she could move more than two or three paces. It wasn't an aggressive hold, more supportive. As if to emphasise this, he patted her elbow and jerked his head back in the direction of the snug at the back.

"Don't be silly. There's no need for politeness around here. Come on. He's a decent man, Garda Conway is. I'm sure he'll tell you what you need."

"Ah, no. I don't want to be any trouble."

"Sure you're not!" Jimmy called over to the corner. "Sure she's not?"

There was a murmur of agreement.

Seanie turned to her and tapped the side of his nose as if letting her in on a secret. "Sure he's three sheets to the wind. He won't even remember telling you anything. Go on there, Fiona. Ask him whatever you want. I'll send over two pints."

And that was how Fiona found herself talking to the man she'd gone there to see in the first place.

12

"I have to hand it to you," Garda Conway said quietly, taking a long sip of his Guinness. "Getting their sympathy and getting them to buy us both a pint? That was a masterstroke."

She shrugged. She wasn't here to talk about her clumsy acting skills and she needed to be quick about it. They thought she was the upset little damsel desperate for information and most of them had been distracted by the darts on the TV, but that wouldn't last for very long.

"I had to. I couldn't raise their suspicions. It would have looked bad if I marched in here and came straight over to you. I haven't been in here for ages."

"So? You're a free agent. You can do what you like."

"I can," she said thoughtfully. "But if rumours were to go round about me talking to you here, I wonder how the sergeant would react to that."

Garda Conway swatted his hand. "I couldn't care less. You know my feelings for that man."

Fiona did—she knew them well. Garda Conway was about as enamoured by his senior officer as Fiona was, and that said a lot.

"Anyway," she said, leaning forward and hoping she didn't look too eager to anyone who might have been watching them. "What's going on over there? Any clue what happened? Is Brennan right, do you think? Was it really a murder?"

Garda Conway took another sip of his pint and reflected on this. After a few moments, he shrugged. "I took the call from the hospital myself. They found definite signs of poisoning."

"But it could be an accident, right?"

He raised his eyebrows. "Maybe if it had happened on a farm or in a factory. But in a pub? Not only that, but in a pub set up like a restaurant where he had gone to celebrate his daughter's wedding? It's highly unlikely, Fiona. I've very sorry to say."

"Any idea when I'll have the pub back?"

It had been at the tip of her tongue to tell him

about the Flanagans, but she just couldn't bring herself to say those words. Stephen Conway was a good man, but this was different. This was a crime. She and Kate had knowingly withheld information.

"I'm afraid not," he said, looking sympathetic. "The lab isn't particularly cooperative. We could be waiting a long time."

She caught the tone in his voice. "You say that like it's unusual."

"Ah," Conway said finishing off the pint in front of him. "These things are changeable. I'm just surprised Brennan hasn't put a rush on it what with his friends in high places."

She winced. "Does that mean he's going to try and point the finger at a local? One of our staff members left before you lot arrived. I suppose he'll be your first suspect."

He stared at her and Fi felt her heart start to pound in her temples.

"I suppose you can't confirm or deny that."

Conway shook his head. "No. We don't have anyone."

"What, Brennan didn't immediately pounce on him for leaving the bar around the time of the murder?"

"No. He had me check it out. Your boy was on break over in Phelan's."

"So why didn't he come back?"

Conway shrugged. "He saw the Garda cars on his way back, I suppose. You can understand it from his point of view. I can at least." He jerked his head to the bar. "Jimmy here confirmed he was in when he said he was in."

He took a drink from his new pint, watching her all the time. She didn't like it. There was something in his eyes.

"What? What is it?"

He put down the glass. "I shouldn't really be telling you this, but since it affects your pub then you have a right to know."

She waited, not wanting to press him.

"Ah I shouldn't say anything at all really. I share your feelings on Brennan but I've still got to think of my job here. And that includes keeping my mouth shut on important matters."

She stared at him, willing him to tell her.

"We have nothing at all," Conway murmured a few moments later.

"What? Nothing? There must be something."

"That's the thing. We've had initial interviews with everyone present that day and we're in the process of talking to them again. It's like a ghost appeared and did it. Apparently it's often someone close to the victim, but in this case his closest family members and friends were with him. They all vouch for each other."

"And you believe them?"

He nodded slowly. "If it was one or two people? Maybe not. But fifty of them saying the same thing?"

Fi grabbed the table. "The cameras! The security cameras in the bar!"

Conway shook his head. "Already been through them."

"But how?" she asked frowning. "I didn't give you the details because I didn't even think of it. Maybe there's a clue on there."

Garda Conway looked sheepish. "The sergeant remembered the cameras from before. I told him it was only right to ask your permission before he went trawling through your laptop. But you know what he's like. Anyway, we were able to get in because you still had the window open; the one that shows the camera feed and history."

Fiona winced. The thought of Sergeant Brennan nosing through her personal files was almost too much to bear. Also disturbing was the fact that she usually left her email account open. What if she'd written something about him in an email he'd discovered?

Garda Conway seemed to sense her concern. "Don't worry. I stayed beside him the whole time he was on your laptop. He opened a couple of photos but otherwise he did nothing but look at the camera footage."

"And there was nothing?"

"I'm afraid not. We looked at it twice and couldn't see any suspicious activity."

Fiona sighed. What did this mean? She closed her eyes and tried to picture the camera angle. Would it have been possible for Mrs Flanagan to sneak downstairs undetected? The camera was angled to show the bar and some of the area beyond it, but it wouldn't show the area where the tables had been set up for dinner. There had been no need to focus the camera on the door that led to the flat because it wasn't really a target.

Which, in Fiona's eyes, seemed like a good explanation for why the guards hadn't found anything. And as time went on, the consequences for her and Kate would become more and more severe.

She shook her head. What was the sense in getting them in legal trouble before she was absolutely certain? She was wavering over whether to tell

Garda Conway, but something held her back. What if she woke in the morning and regretted it? There'd be no way to take it back. Plus, she couldn't exactly tell him in Phelan's—if he hurried out the door then it would cause no end of gossip in the town. Everyone would think—rightly—that she knew more than she was letting on.

"There must be something," she said, trying to keep the desperation out of her voice.

"No." He shook his head. "We've got pretty much nothing."

"Pretty much nothing?"

He shook his head. "It must have been one of those guests, but so far none of them is striking us as having something to hide."

She frowned. "And the staff? Why hadn't he hauled us in there to interrogate us?"

Garda Conway threw his head back and laughed. "The one time he's not going on a witch hunt after a local and you're complaining about it?"

"You're right. Nobody here knew the man so what reason would they have had to kill him? Though I suppose they might have recognised him from years ago."

"Is that so?"

She nodded. "He used to be a famous showband singer."

Garda Conway frowned. "Was he? That's funny. I didn't recognise him, but sure I suppose…"

He shrugged.

"It must be hard," she mused. "Trying to find a murderer in a crowd who've left town."

"Ah not at all," the Garda said cheerily. "We were lucky to get there fast and contain the situation. We've accounted for everyone in that room. We may not have found the suspect yet, but it's a numbers game. We'll find out what happened sooner or later."

Fiona nodded, trying to look calm. Inside she was anything but positive. Now it felt like she and her sister were only delaying the inevitable firestorm of trouble they'd somehow gotten themselves into.

There was no suspect—because they'd failed to tell the guards about the two women who'd been upstairs and unaccounted for that afternoon.

13

Fiona's parents, sister and brothers were crowded into the sitting room watching TV when she arrived home. She was met with a barrage of questions—her father even grabbed the remote and muted the TV in order to allow her to answer them all.

Fi sighed. If she asked to speak to Kate in private, she'd only raise their suspicions. She answered their questions patiently. When they were satisfied, she crossed the room and sat on the floor in front of her sister.

She waited five minutes.

"Hey Kate?"

"What?"

"Do you have a hair straightener?"

Fi felt her sister move behind her.

"Course I do. What are you talking about? My hair'd look as bad as yours if I didn't straighten it every day."

Ouch.

Fi ignored the insult. "Ah great. Can I borrow it?"

"Yeah if you want."

"Can you get it for me?"

"Why? Have you lost the use of your arms and legs? Go get it yourself."

"I don't know where it is."

"It's on my dresser."

"But sure that's a mess."

Kate wasn't to be moved from the couch and Fi was out of ideas. She left and headed upstairs to her sister's room.

She clicked her tongue when she saw the chaos that was the top of her sister's dresser. If she'd actually wanted to use her sister's straightener then she'd have had a hard time finding in the chaos of makeup, discarded clothes and old food containers.

She pulled out her phone and sent her sister a message.

Don't say anything. Get up here. Need to talk ASAP!

Then she waited while Kate took her sweet time to leave the sitting room and come upstairs.

"Why couldn't you just tell me what you wanted downstairs?" Kate said sullenly. "My feet are tired from running around all day."

"Poor you. Look, we need to talk about what happened with Mrs Flanagan."

"Why? It's not your problem. I'm dealing with it. I'm hoping Marie's going to change her mind."

Fi shook her head. "That's not why I wanted to talk to you. I went to Phelan's to see Garda Conway."

"And?"

"And he says they're at a loss. That they assume it's one of the guests but they haven't found any clues. It's an out-of-towner from the wedding, they just don't know who."

"That's good."

"Is it?" Fi plonked herself down on the messy bed. Their mother had given up trying to keep it tidy a long time ago. "I don't think so. It means we might get into trouble for failing to tell them about the Flanagans being upstairs."

"Why would we get into trouble? Anyway, what do you care? You've been clashing with Brennan ever since he got here. What's one more fight?"

"You really don't get it, do you? This isn't

Brennan going off on some power trip. This is serious. There's a Garda investigation into a murder that happened in my pub. The Flanagans were there and we still haven't told the guards that."

"The Flanagans aren't murderers. They're my clients."

"They've got nobody else. They have to be involved in this."

Kate pursed her lips. "That makes no sense. Why would they book a wedding only to then turn around and murder someone in the same venue? It'd be crazy."

"Think about it. They now want to cancel the wedding," Fiona said, leaning closer to her sister. "Maybe that was the intention all along."

"What do you mean? They can't have known Kilcomer's daughter was getting married."

"Why not?"

"Because of the confidentiality agreement, remember?"

Fi waved her hand dismissively. "Sure that means nothing. That covered *you*. Any one of the guests could have told people they were going to that wedding. When did Mrs Flanagan first approach you about coming along to it?"

"It was my idea for them to come along, Fi! You

were there. Do you not remember? Are you losing the plot?"

Fi shook her head. Truth be told, she wasn't sure if she was losing the plot or not. There was certainly a strong possibility.

"We're getting distracted. The important thing is we knew they were there and we said nothing. That's going to get us into trouble when the guards finally find something that points to Mrs Flanagan."

Kate leapt forward with a gasp. "What are you saying?!"

"I'm saying there's a possibility that Mrs Flanagan's our murderer."

"Yeah, just like there's a possibility one of us is the murderer. It's unlikely. What reason did she have to kill him? She didn't even know him!"

"But she did, Kate," Fi said slowly as she tried to recount the events of that day. "Remember? She fainted. And the way she looked at him when we were going upstairs. It wasn't normal, Kate. It certainly wasn't the way you'd look at a guy you didn't know."

"No, Fi. You can't be serious. You're accusing my client of murder. They may have asked to cancel the contract, but until I agree they're still my clients."

"They don't need your agreement! They could just sue you!"

"It won't come to that. I'll chat with Marie. I'll convince her to stick with us. What you're saying could ruin me. The wedding planner who accused her client of murder? I'll never book another function again if I... Have you said anything to the guards?"

"No," Fi said quietly. "I wanted to but I bottled it. I was too unsure. But now..."

Kate's eyes widened to the size of saucers. "Now?"

Fi shook her head. "The more I think about it, the more certain I get. It was so strange. Maybe she even pretended to faint knowing we'd take her upstairs. Anyway, I don't know the details. I just know we need to take this to the guards."

"Tell me you're not serious!" Kate howled.

"I've never been more serious. We can't keep this to ourselves anymore. Not when doing so could get us into a whole lot of trouble. We could be accessories to murder."

The door burst open and Margaret McCabe stormed in. Her face was red with fury. Fiona's heart sank. She should have suspected this.

"How long have you been listening at the door, Mam?"

"Long enough! Accessories to murder! My goodness! And ye keeping it to yourselves? Well not on my watch! You're to get yourselves down to the Garda station right this minute, do you hear me?"

IN THE END, they managed to calm Mrs McCabe down but she was still adamant that they had to go to the Garda station the next day. Fiona was fine with that. She wasn't keen on going there in the middle of the night, which would have required them to call the out-of-hours number and state the reason for their visit in order to arrange for one of the guards to meet them there.

The less official their visit was, the better.

14

Fiona woke earlier than usual. Her mother had wanted her to sleep on an airbed in her sister's room, but she much preferred the couch. She'd told them she'd be glad of the space once they were sharing a prison cell for the next ten years.

Neither her mother nor her sister had found it particularly amusing. Probably because they didn't allow hair straighteners in prisons. She didn't know. She didn't know anything about prisons.

She shivered. She was wide awake now and she'd succeeded in scaring the hell out of herself by thinking about jail. She'd only been joking the night before.

But was it a possibility?

After all, Brennan had managed to get Dec Hanlon imprisoned for several months because he hadn't paid his TV licence. Why did she doubt that he'd do the same to her for withholding vital information in a case?

That settled it. She jumped out of her sleeping bag and hurried upstairs. She didn't care if they had to wait outside the door of the Garda station until it opened. They were going there. And they were going to speak to Garda Conway and hope that he could ease their statement into evidence in a way that didn't set Brennan on their path.

What was the alternative? Allow a murderer to get off scot-free? She couldn't have that on her conscience.

Fi hurried up the stairs, taking them two at a time and not paying any attention to the noise she was making. This was too urgent. She was sure her family would understand—none of them would be too keen on making weekly trips to Mountjoy to visit her.

She hurried along the landing, ignoring her father's shouts to be quiet. Kate's was the room at the end. She threw the door open and barged inside.

"Kate, wake up. Come on."

The lump in the bed didn't move. She stared at it impatiently.

She marched across the room and shook the

lump where she thought her sister's shoulders must be.

They were remarkably soft and pliable for shoulders.

Fi groaned and pulled the covers back, finding herself faced with a pile of pillows that definitely wasn't her younger sister.

"Kate?"

At first she thought it was a prank, though she failed to see why Kate would find it remotely funny. She checked the wardrobe and the blanket box at the end of her sister's bed. They were messy and chaotic, but Kate wasn't in either of them. Nor was she in the upstairs or downstairs bathroom, or in any of the other rooms.

By the time Fi was finished looking for her, she was sure of two things: her family wouldn't forgive her for disturbing them at such an early hour and Kate absolutely wasn't in the house.

Fi was standing halfway down the stairs wondering what to do when her mother emerged from her room in the process of tying her shocking pink dressing gown tightly around herself.

"Do you want some breakfast, love? What are you doing waking up the whole house?"

Fi shook her head slowly, still working through

the scenario in her tired brain. "I don't know, Mam. Kate's gone. I came up to get her up to go to the Garda station. You know; what we talked about last night."

Margaret's eyes lit up like a lightbulb had just gone on inside her head. "Ah, yes. Of course."

"Well did you hear her get up?"

"No I didn't. I was out like a light until you barged into our room and started opening the wardrobe doors."

"She's gone, Mam. She's gone but she was supposed to come with me."

"Maybe she left already."

Fi considered the possibility for a moment and then dismissed it. "When have you ever known Kate to do anything first thing in the morning?"

Her mother shrugged. "She's been different lately. Proactive."

That was true. After all, she'd surprised Fi with the level of planning and thought that had gone into the weddings. Sure, the murder might mean she didn't make as much of a profit, but that was outside of Kate's control. If she hadn't faced that snag then she would have made a fortune off the events.

"Come on, love. Come and have some breakfast."

"No, Mam. I should go down to the station and

meet her there." She didn't say what else she was thinking—that she wouldn't put it past Kate to try and make a deal for herself while landing Fi in serious trouble.

BUT IT TURNED out that her sister's loyalty was the least of Fi's worries. There was nobody at the Garda station, which was still closed. Fi checked all around the building and scanned the shops across the road. There was no sign of her.

She shook her head. Where else could Kate have possibly gone if she wasn't home and she wasn't outside the Garda station?

She started walking back home, thinking she might take her mother up on the idea of breakfast after all.

Then she stopped.

She knew Kate. Old Kate; new Kate; it didn't matter. Kate was Kate. And Kate would protect her money over anything else.

She turned and broke into a run, heading straight for the train station.

"Here! You can't just barge in here without showing your ticket."

Fi stopped and stared at the man. He looked vaguely familiar. But then it was Ballycashel, and everybody knew everyone else at least to see if not by name.

"I don't have one. I'm looking for my sister. I need to stop her."

The man relaxed and shook his head. "What's your hurry? The next train's not until half eight."

"And the one to Dublin?"

"That's the one I'm talking about."

Fi sighed. "Can I just check the platform to see if she's there?"

"No point, love," he said with the same unhurried lilt. "Train to and from Dublin left about ten and fifteen minutes ago. Nobody's there now. You'd be mad to wait in the cold for over an hour."

"The waiting room?" she asked, pointing in its direction.

He laughed. "About as comfortable as waiting outside. No, you won't find anyone in there either." He narrowed his eyes and leant closer to her. "You're Francis McCabe's girl, aren't you?"

She nodded.

"The one with the funny notion about opening a fancy pub here in town."

Fi rolled her eyes. There was a certain faction in town who'd never forgive her for moving away from the traditional pub model. Someday she hoped to prove them wrong by becoming rich beyond her wildest dreams, but it didn't look like that would happen soon.

"Yeah that's me," she said quietly.

"I thought so," he said nodding. "You have the look of him. And you're looking for your sister, you say."

"That's right. I don't know if she came here but she doesn't drive." She wouldn't have got the bus, Fi knew, because Kate hated buses. She point blank refused to get on them unless she was away from Ballycashel, and even then she wouldn't use them if there was any alternative way of getting around.

The man nodded slowly. "Do you know, there was a lassie in this morning I don't see here every day. I thought I knew her from somewhere. Francis's other girl I suppose."

"Was it? Are you sure?"

He shrugged. "Can never be sure of anything. She looked like you. Unfriendly. In a hurry."

"What time was that at?"

"Oh, early," he said. "She just made the six o'clock."

"To Dublin?"

"Well that's the only six o'clock train around here," he said as if it was obvious.

Fiona wasn't listening. Her heart had leapt into her throat and was hammering so hard it felt like it might explode. It was nearly half seven now. Kate had a whole hour and a half headstart and that was before even considering the extra hour Fi would lose waiting for the next train.

"You're sure there's no train before half eight?"

He squinted. "I've been working here twenty years. Course I'm sure."

She thanked him and took off out of the station at a sprint.

15

She ran straight to Marty's house. This was an emergency. It didn't matter that she was wearing a pair of old tracksuit bottoms from her school days paired with a ratty t-shirt and an old hoodie of Ben's—she had more important things on her mind.

Like Kate.

Her stupid sister was walking straight into the hands of a potential murderer.

What was she thinking?

It was about a kilometre and a half to Marty's from the train station and Fi was gasping for breath by the time she ran up the path and hammered on the door. She hadn't run so far since... well, she couldn't remember ever running that far.

But it didn't matter. Kate might have been the biggest thorn in her side, but she was also her sister.

And sisters didn't let sister go off and get murdered if they could help it.

"Come onnnn!" she shouted, aware of the neighbours' net curtains twitching all around her.

Colm came to the door a few moments later. "Fi," he said sleepily. "What's up? What are you doing here so early?"

"Marty!" she cried. "Marty! Need car!"

It took him a few moments to get what she was saying—she wasn't exactly coherent in her current state. "Ah he's gone. You've missed him. He's at the shop."

Fi didn't move. She should have known, but she'd lost track of time and everything else in the moments since she learnt of Kate's foolish trip to Dublin. "Keys. Give me the keys."

Colm shook his head. "What keys?"

"The keys to Marty's car! Come on! We don't have time!"

This, of course, piqued Colm's curiosity. He hurried to get the keys, but before he handed them to her, he demanded she tell him what was going on.

Which wouldn't have been a problem, except she

didn't have a short version of the story she could tell him.

"We don't have time," she wailed. "I need to go!"

"Wait a sec."

"I can't! Where are you going? I need to go now!"

He returned a moment later, throwing his arms into his thick black coat. "I'll go with you. You can tell me in the car."

She sighed gratefully and hurried after him to the old station wagon. Colm had always been the reckless boy racer of the family. She usually tried to avoid being in cars with him, but this time was an exception. She couldn't have picked anyone better to drive unless she'd had her choice of rally drivers.

* * *

WHAT FIONA HADN'T FACTORED in, of course, was traffic on the motorway. Ballycashel was a bit too far away to be considered a true commuter town, but some of the towns further up the motorway were mainly populated by people who worked in the city and drove up and down every day.

It was just after eight by then, probably the worst possible time for trying to get to Dublin. They rolled along, not quite bumper-to-bumper, but not going at speed either. At the rate they were going, it'd take another hour and a half to get there, though she knew things would clear up and start moving eventually.

"Where are we going?" Colm asked. "I know we're going to this woman's house, but where exactly is it? It'd help if we could get off this road before the city centre. Might buy us half an hour or so."

It was only then that the reality of what they were doing set in.

What are we at? she thought frantically as they crawled along the motorway, surrounded by commuters off to office jobs. *We've got to help Kate, but... this?*

Thinking about it didn't calm her in the slightest. In fact, the more she thought about it, the more she came to the conclusion that they were absolute nutcases to be rushing into the unknown like this.

"Colm, what are we doing?"

He glanced at her. Traffic was stopping and starting, so if he took his eyes off the road for longer than a split second there was a good chance he might end up in the back of somebody else's car.

"What do you mean, what are we doing? We're going to Dublin because you arrived over in your...

whatever you're wearing and demanded to take the car."

"You said you'd drive me."

"I wasn't going to let you go off on your own in that state. Of course I did. I'm your brother."

Hearing that made tears well up in her eyes— and she wasn't usually the sentimental type. It was more to do with the stress of the situation, she reasoned.

"I think we're making a big mistake. We've got to get to Kate and make sure she's alright, but she had such a headstart on us. What if it's too late and we're just walking into trouble?"

He looked at her quickly and then turned his attention back to the road, frowning. "I suppose it's a risk we're going to have to take. What I can't understand is why you didn't go to the guards in the first place."

"We were going to do it this morning."

He groaned. "I don't know what's wrong with this family thinking they can go off and solve crimes and save the world. I think I preferred the lazy Kate who could barely be relied on to feed herself never mind start a business."

"I'm starting to think you're right. But that doesn't help us now. What are we going to do? Knock on the door and tell them to leave our sister out of it?"

"Are you sure that's where she's gone? She couldn't just be off... I dunno... shopping?"

"Please. Do you really think she's changed that much? I've never known her to go shopping so early, not even when the Christmas sales are on. No, she's gone to the Flanagans. That has to be it. She was dead against the idea of going to the guards but I insisted we had to." She slapped her forehead with her palm. "Why did I say anything to her? So stupid! I just needed to know I wasn't being absolutely crazy."

"You should have come to one of the rest of us instead. From what you've told me, your one Mrs Flanagan sounds like the only plausible suspect they've got. Only they don't know it yet."

Fiona swallowed. "And they don't know where we've gone. If we end up like that man... Colm, there's nobody to find us."

He shook his head. "Don't say that. There's two of us. We'll be grand."

She stared out the window. Traffic was beginning to ease up a bit, though it was still heavy. She tried to picture the situation. Mrs Flanagan had struck her as a rich suburban woman. None of it made sense.

Surely the wife of a prominent solicitor wouldn't risk her reputation to kill a man.

But then people acted irrationally all the time. And there had been something in her eyes when she looked at that man.

And maybe it was even more worrying that her husband was so well-regarded. They had a lot more to lose when the truth came out.

Had Kate even considered that for a moment before she went skipping off to Dublin?

Fiona gripped the dashboard in front of her. "Colm, can you pull off at the next service station?"

There was only one thing she could do. She didn't like it, but she had to do it.

16

"Are you going to tell me what we're doing here?"

Fi shook her head. "Hang on. I'm trying to convince myself this is the right thing to do."

"Fi, you're confusing me here. One minute we had to get to Dublin as quickly as possible, the next you're making me pull off here and sit around in the car. Have you heard something? Is Kate okay?"

"I wish I knew. I've been trying to ring her but she's not answering her phone."

"Doesn't that make this even more urgent? They could have her in a situation where she's not able to get to her phone."

That settled it for Fi. So what if they got in trouble if it meant her sister was safe? She hit the number she'd pulled up from her phone contacts.

A gruff voice answered a short while later.

"Garda Conway," she said urgently. "It's me, Fiona. If you're in company don't say anything. Just listen to me."

"Fi…" he cleared his throat. "Feeeine. That's…ahem… fine."

"So the sarge is with you?"

"Yes, Sergeant Brennan is here, Mrs Hennessy. But I don't think he'll be able to offer any more assistance in finding your cat than I can offer."

She heard a sharp voice in the background and smiled to herself. "Good recovery."

"Yes well, there's life in the old dog yet. Ah yes, that's insensitive of me. Yes, I realise that. Your cat is precious. Of course. Yes."

"It's about the case," Fi hissed. "Can you meet us at the big service station on the M5? Exit…" she looked around frantically. "Exit nine."

There was a silence on the other end of the line. "Are you serious?"

"I'm afraid so. Look, I can't explain it all on the phone. But you have to believe me. We're on to something."

"Can't it wait?"

"No. Definitely not. Please, just get here as soon as possible."

"Fine," he said, sounding resentful. "I don't suppose you have a ladder?"

"Who was that?"

"Don't worry, it was Conway. I had to tell him, it's too serious not to."

"What's he going to do that we can't do? He's due to retire soon."

She shrugged helplessly. "So? He's a Garda. He's trained. And I'm hoping he has contacts in other stations he can call in to help us once we've assessed the situation."

"You're stone mad," Colm said, shaking his head. "I'm going in to get a breakfast roll. You want one?"

"Yeah go on so," she said, pulling up the maps app on her phone. "It'll take him a while. I'll have a jambon. Just make sure it's not one of those vegetable ones. I got one of them by mistake last time. It was disgusting."

She remembered Kate mentioning the Flanagan's big house in Dundrum, but as soon as she looked at the map she knew it was hopeless without having at least a street name. And none of the streets radiating out from the town centre struck her as familiar.

Sighing, she opened the web browser and tapped in 'Flanagan solicitor'. There were too many results to be useful and she couldn't remember the man's first name. She tapped on the *news* search, but she knew it was pointless. She didn't have time to scroll through the results to find out which ones were crime reports from the courts and which might be more to do with social events than legal matters.

There was only one thing for it.

She opened her email app and found the last email Kate had sent about the wedding planning. Fi hadn't paid much attention to the actual email address her sister was using—now she prayed it was the same webmail account she'd always had and not an email address associated with her new website. If it was the latter, Fiona had no clue how to access it.

She breathed a sigh of relief when she saw it. It was the same as always.

She wasn't home and dry yet. She went back and selected the option to add a new account to her phone. It felt very strange doing so, but the circumstances weren't exactly normal. Plus she'd done the exact same thing before in a less urgent situation.

She just hoped Kate hadn't suddenly decided to become internet savvy. It wouldn't doom them, exactly, but it might slow them down.

But no, Kate hadn't paid attention to any of the many warnings her family had given her. Her password was still katemcabe, just like the last time Fi had tried it. Her triumph was tinged with regret that her sister was so irresponsible, especially now she was running a business and invoicing people for a lot of money.

Her regret was short-lived, though. She tapped 'flanagan' into the search bar and soon came up with a series of emails back and forth with Marie. She scanned the right-hand side, looking for any messages with attachments. There were none.

She returned to the top and searched 'flanagan invoice'. There was nothing. She shook her head. How was her sister billing people? She remembered Kate's words then. She'd mentioned a contract; she'd definitely mentioned a contract.

'Flanagan contract' pulled up no results, but then she tried contract on its own and several emails were listed. She shook her head in astonishment. There were at least fifteen between Kate and their parents' solicitor, probably agreeing on the wording.

That gave her some consolation about her sister's business savvy, though it didn't exactly help their situation now. She scanned through the list and her eyes landed on an email from Marie Flanagan.

Yes! Fi knew Marie still lived with her parents—Kate had wondered aloud on many occasions how she and her future husband could stand living in the same house as Mrs Flanagan.

And the address was listed. Fi took a screenshot of the contract page and rummaged in the glove box for a pen. She scribbled the address on the back of her hand just in case her battery died. It was at 88%, but she didn't want to leave anything to chance.

By the time Colm returned from the shop with a large paper bag and a tray of coffees, Fi had tapped the address into maps and was ready to go.

She glanced at the clock.

It was only fifteen minutes since she called Garda Conway.

"Thanks," she said, taking the coffees from her brother to allow him to climb back into the car. "How long does it normally take to get here from Ballycashel?"

"It took us half an hour."

"In normal traffic?"

He glanced toward the road, which was just about visible from where they were parked. "Maybe twenty minutes? Twenty-five?"

She ate her jambon in silence, pausing only to take sips of her coffee. She regretted her haste a minute later when she was wiping her hands on the rough napkin that had come in the bag. Now she had nothing to distract her until Conway arrived.

She took her seatbelt off and turned around in her seat, staring at the slip road that came off the motorway and led to the carpark.

"Come on," she muttered.

"He'll be a while yet," Colm muttered, mouth still full of breakfast roll. "Calm down."

"I can't," she said, tapping her fingers on the plastic console between the two seats. "I'll try Kate again."

There was still no answer. She cursed and returned her attention to her phone, staring at the route between their present location and the Flanagans' home until she felt sure she could recite it from memory.

She found herself at a loss again. Colm was still eating.

"Let's play I spy. I spy with my little eye, something beginning with... 'T'."

Colm looked at her, then he threw a glance out the windscreen. "Truck," he said immediately.

"I gave you that one on a plate. Okay, I spy—"

"Ah come on, Fi. We're not eight."

"I need a way of distracting myself."

"We'll go over to the carwash then. You can clean out the car and pick up all those crumbs you've dropped all over the place."

"I would but we need to be ready to go."

The minutes crawled by. The car felt like it was closing in on them. She was tempted to call Garda Conway but logic told her to leave it. What was the sense in annoying him when he'd told her he was on his way?

Finally when she could almost no longer bear the waiting—even though she knew only a few minutes had passed—the sound of sirens echoed around the carpark, which was located in a natural valley.

She stared in astonishment. "It's him! Please tell me it's him!"

It could have been any of the thousands of other guards in the country, of course. She knew that. And she also knew that Garda Conway had come even though he wasn't supposed to, so he'd hardly be advertising that fact.

Then the Garda car pulled up alongside them and she saw a frazzled-looking Stephen Conway in the driver's seat.

Fi leapt out of the car faster than she'd ever moved in her whole life.

17

To her surprise, Garda Conway didn't dismiss her suspicions. Instead, he waited until she'd finished her story and then shook his head.

"You should have come to us. She had no reason to go off and try to solve this on her own."

"She wasn't thinking. She was just trying to protect her client. I'm to blame. I should have seen this coming."

"You're both to blame, but there's no time to sit around and throw accusations around. We need to get going."

"So you believe me? You don't think this is a needle in a haystack?"

"No," he said soberly. "No, it sounds far more promising than anything else we've found. At first I thought it must be family—Brennan's still sure it is, but they're not saying anything. Have you got the address?"

She nodded.

"Right so. Let's go."

GARDA CONWAY TURNED on the sirens again and they raced up the motorway. He was going so fast that Fi's knuckles turned white from clinging to the handle above her door.

In no time at all, they were across the M50 and taking the exit for Dundrum. Fi turned on GPS and navigated Conway through the streets.

"Wait," she said. "Shouldn't you get Garda backup or something?"

"Are you joking me? We're going straight into Brennan's territory. You know who his father is. I'm not risking that."

"I'm sorry to put you in this position, but isn't it better to be safe?"

Conway looked at her and smiled. She wanted to tell him to look back at the road, but she held off. He'd been driving at speeds like this since before she was born. He had this. She wasn't sure she could say the same about their plan to just storm the Flanagan house.

"Don't you go worrying now. I never said we had to go in there alone."

"But you just did."

He tapped the side of his nose. "You just wait and see. But don't worry now."

Within a few minutes, they were pulling onto the Flanagans' road. Garda Conway had long since turned off the siren to allow them as much of an element of surprise as possible. He drove past the house and glanced at it a few times before pulling up on a side street about a hundred metres past it.

He killed the engine.

Fi looked back at Colm, who shrugged. She had butterflies in her stomach now and a huge sense of dread. This was serious; easily the most serious situation they'd ever been in. What made it worse was that one of their family was quite likely in there alone.

"Right, come on."

Garda Conway climbed out of the car and walked in the opposite direction, away from the house. He stopped to talk to two men in fleece jackets, jeans and runners, standard uniform for retired Irish men of a certain age who liked to stay active.

"They're guards," Colm hissed. "Look at them."

She looked more closely at them this time and saw what he meant. She could imagine either of them in uniform. There was just a certain air about them.

Garda Conway gestured them over.

"This is John and Maurice. They're going to help us today."

Both men nodded simultaneously, jutting their chins up in the exact same way.

"Thank you," Fi said gratefully. "It's my sister in there."

"Don't you worry about her. Just do what this man says and everything'll be grand."

"Ye checked the back way?"

One of the men nodded. "We did. The back garden is all walled off. No way in from that side."

"Anything we should be worried about?"

"There's a side door. We'll keep an eye on it."

"Right so. You cover that. I'll go round the front."

They decided after a lot of back and forth that it was best if the men hid and allowed Fi to knock on the door first, to make it seem as if she was there alone. That way, they'd avoid any repercussions for Kate of her captors being put under pressure.

It was risky and Colm didn't like it, but Fi didn't

even hesitate before agreeing. After all, it was she who'd pushed Kate to travel here in the first place by telling her she was going to the guards.

That didn't mean she was particularly relaxed. There was no car outside the big semi-detached house, which made her worry that they'd taken off somewhere with Kate. It also meant there was no cover for Garda Conway and Colm to use as they snuck up the driveway. The only option was for them to walk as briskly and silently as they could and step aside at the last minute. Luckily there were prominent windowsills on either side, giving them some cover to crouch under and remain unseen if anyone looked out the windows.

When they were out of the way, Fiona knocked loudly on the door, far louder than was considered polite. With any luck, the disturbance would cause the neighbours to look out in disgust. That was the plan anyway. Make it so that any murderous actions would have to be done in full view of Mrs Flanagan's neighbours, because she seemed like the sort of woman who very much cared what the neighbours thought.

Nobody came to the door. At first she was disheartened—after all, wouldn't Mrs Flanagan do her damnedest to avoid a scene—but she pushed that thought to the back of her mind and knocked even harder.

"Open the door, please. It's Fiona McCabe. I need to see my sister."

She kept knocking and shouting. She couldn't see the neighbour's houses because of the depth of the porch, but she hoped they were like her neighbours in Ballycashel—motivated to snoop by the slightest hint of unusual activity.

Finally she saw someone approach through the tinted glass of the front door. "Someone's coming," she hissed as quietly as she could.

Colm and the Garda shuffled forward a few inches, readying themselves to leap up.

The door opened. Fiona found herself looking into the face of Marie Flanagan, who stared back cheerfully as if they weren't a bunch of murderers.

"Where's my sister?" Fi demanded.

Marie smiled. "She's just inside."

Her stomach churned with loathing. Did it not even bother them in the slightest what they were doing?

"Is she alright? She better be."

"Of course she is. We need her alive, don't we?" she said, laughing coldly.

Fi pursed her lips. "You better not have hurt her."

"Ah, Mam knocked her down a bit but she'll live."

She couldn't stand it anymore. Garda Conway had warned her to keep things calm if she could and not escalate the situation, but this was taking it a bit too far."

"You smug so-and-so!" she leapt forward, pushing through the door before Marie had a chance to act. Colm and Garda Conway were on their feet in seconds, hurrying in behind her. Garda Conway muttered something into his phone as they moved, telling the other two men what was going on.

"Mammy! Mammy!" Marie cried from behind them.

Her shrieks only spurred them on to move faster, fearful of what the woman might do now that they were caught.

18

"Get off her! Get off her now!"

The new arrivals stopped and blinked, taking in what they were seeing.

On first glance, it had looked like Mrs Flanagan had Kate in some kind of chokehold. After all, the two women had their backs to them on the low-backed chaise longue that was dwarfed by the vastness of the plush living room.

Now that they were closer, though, they got a better sense of what was going on.

Mrs Flanagan hadn't moved; hadn't put her hands in the air. Instead she sat frozen, staring at Garda Conway as if she'd never been so frightened in her life.

Not only that, but it was becoming increasingly clear that Kate had been holding Mrs Flanagan, not the other way around. And far from looking relieved, Kate seemed absolutely furious.

"What's going on?" Marie cried, following them into the room. "Who are you people? What do you want? If it's jewellery, then help yourselves." She turned and looked at Fiona with disappointment in her eyes. "I can't believe this. I trusted you. You seemed so nice."

Fiona was too surprised to respond. They were accusing her of being a criminal when it was the other way around?

Kate had leapt to her feet by now and hurried to Marie's side. The young woman was staring at her uncertainly.

"Were you in on this too?"

Kate flung her hands out. "They're not trying to rob you. No! This is all about what happened at that wedding. I should have known my sister would freak out and do something like this."

"The wedding? They're here because Mammy fainted?"

Kate shook her head and squeezed her temples.

Fiona looked from Kate to Marie and shook her head. "What? Don't tell me you're going to try and act all innocent—"

Garda Conway stepped forward. He cleared his

throat. "I take it you're Mrs Flanagan. This young lady says she has reason to believe you were—"

They were interrupted by a sharp knock on the door. Marie turned to go answer it and Garda Conway followed close behind her.

The wait was agonising. Fiona stared at Mrs Flanagan, unwilling to let the woman out of her sight lest she try and escape. It galled her that her own sister had sat there and warned the woman. Was there anything Kate wouldn't do for her business?

They could hear men's voices from outside, punctuated by Conway's quiet, calm voice. It felt like an age had passed by the time he returned to the room. Marie looked even more solemn than before. Her hands were shaking, even though she'd clasped them tightly in front of her.

Nobody spoke.

What was going on? Fi could only conclude that the Flanagans had fed Kate a whole load of lies and she'd believed them rather than upsetting a client.

Suddenly Fiona couldn't wait anymore. She needed to know. "Kate, will you please tell me what's going on? You know what we spoke about last night. Next thing I knew you were running off to Dublin on your own. I thought you were in trouble!"

Kate stared at her sullenly. "You didn't have to follow me here."

"Of course I did! I thought you were walking right into the hands of a murderer! What was I going to do, just go about my business?"

Kate clicked her tongue scornfully.

"A murderer? What is she talking about Kate?" Marie hissed.

Kate's shoulders slumped. "My sister thinks your mam's a murderer."

Fi glared at her.

Fortunately Garda Conway chose that moment to step in. "It's come to my attention, Mrs Flanagan, that you were at McCabe's bar in Ballycashel when a Mr Patrick Kilcomer was murdered. You had a fainting fit and were brought upstairs. Is that correct?"

Mrs Flanagan, now pale and far from her usual haughty self, nodded. "Yes."

"I see. And was there a reason for your fainting spell?"

"She just fainted. I don't see how that makes her a criminal."

"Answer the question, please."

"You can't just question her without her solicitor

present. It's not right. If my father knew about this—"

"Miss Flanagan, your mother was present in the building when a murder took place. When Miss McCabe went to check on her she was gone and that was shortly after the murder. I have a witness who claims that your mother fainted shortly after the victim entered the bar and then proceeded to point him out in the crowd when she passed him later that afternoon. Now." He clasped his hands together. "What's a reasonable person supposed to make of that? Everyone else in the building was a friend, a relative, or a member of staff to whom the victim was previously unknown."

"I was with her!" the usually calm Marie cried. "We left that flat because Mam felt fine but she was eager to get home to her own bed after seeing that man. Isn't that right, Mam? We knew nothing about a murder."

But Mrs Flanagan said nothing. She was staring at Garda Conway with a funny look in her eyes similar to the way she'd looked at Kilcomer on the day of the murder.

"He's not who he claims to be. I know that for a fact."

"Mam!"

"What's your history with him? How do you know the man?"

"Excuse me, Garda! You can't question her without her having legal representation. She's in no fit state—"

"Did you know him from his showband days?" Fi interrupted. She needed to know. The whole mess wasn't showing any signs of clearing itself up anytime soon.

"I'm going to have to insist—"

But Mrs Flanagan was more eager to talk than her daughter realised. She blinked and shook her head as if she'd been woken from her trance. "Show-band? Showband? Is that what they're calling it these days?"

"That's what they've always called it," Fi said impatiently. "Singer. Band member. Showband. Whatever you want to call it. According to my sister, he was quite a famous singer back in the day. We thought that might be how you knew him."

The woman's face screwed up in disgust. "You think he's a singer? Good God, what have you taken? That man's no famous singer. Are you telling me you have no idea who he really is? What kind of a Garda are you?"

19

Fiona was now more bewildered than ever. Luckily, Garda Conway seemed to take Mrs Flanagan's strange statement in his stride.

"What are you telling me, Madam?" he asked gently, pointing to the couch opposite the one Kate and Mrs Flanagan had been sitting on before all of the mayhem kicked off. The woman nodded and he sat down. Fi scuttled over and joined him, wishing she was anywhere but there.

"Fine, I suppose I'd better make a cup of tea if we're doing this," Marie said, shaking her head in disbelief.

Her mother nodded slowly, still deathly pale. "Yes, love. Please do. It seems we have a few things to clear up. Garda, did you really think I was the murderer?"

Colm and Garda Conway's two companions slipped out of the house after getting a subtle nod from him. It was becoming clear that Mrs Flanagan wasn't a threat to anyone. "It seems we may have had a misunderstanding. I'm not here to persecute you. But I need to know what happened. It's clear that you knew the man and that you didn't hold him in particularly high regard."

"High regard?" she muttered. "High regard? He's nothing but a gangster."

"How exactly do you know him, Mrs Flanagan?"

"Oh God bless us and save us," she muttered, reaching over to take a tissue from the decorative box on an occasional table. "I suppose I'd better tell you what I've already told Kate. Marie was only trying to protect me, you know."

She blew her nose and elegantly deposited the rolled up tissue in her sleeve.

"Go on. I promise you, we won't mention a word of what you say to anyone, unless we have reason to believe that doing so can prevent further injury to anyone or might help us in convicting a criminal. Do you understand?"

Mrs Flanagan nodded. "Yes, yes I do. And I needn't worry so. I have no idea who killed him.

Though if I were you, I'd prepare myself for making a very long list."

Fiona stared bewildered at Garda Conway. Surely if there was something so dodgy about their victim, the guards would have realised it by now? How was it that Mrs Flanagan supposedly knew the truth when they were in the dark?

"Tell me everything you know about him, Mrs Flanagan," Garda Conway said, taking a notebook and pen from his pocket.

She nodded, staring at her hands and seemingly struggling to get her thoughts in order. "Okay. Well." She shook her head and laughed nervously. "There's no particularly easy way of saying it." She glanced around looking hunted.

Things were going from strange to stranger, she reflected. It was clear that Mrs Flanagan had something to hide, but it didn't appear that she was the murderer. So what was it? She seemed almost *sheepish*.

Mrs Flanagan hung her head after taking another tissue from the box. This time she didn't use it, she merely worried it between her fingers. She hadn't struck Fi as a fidgeter, rather as a woman with supreme self-control.

It was clear that Fi's assessment had been incorrect.

"It was years back. I haven't thought about him for at least ten years." She sighed heavily, like a woman who had the weight of the world on her shoulders. "I'd finally forgotten him. Our paths couldn't have gone in more different ways. I was the girl from the council estate turned good. I went back and did my leaving. Went to college. Met Fintan." She laughed mirthlessly. "Even went and got elocution lessons at Fintan's mother's insistence. You know, to take the edge off.

"Well anyway, I was sixteen at the time. He was eighteen. Oh I thought he was so flash. He had a car, you see. Ah it wasn't just that. He was the tough guy around the estate. There's always one of them." She looked up at them, beseeching them to understand. "The fearless fella who'll jump that bit farther; fight the lad who's twice his size. That was Pa Kilcomer."

"How did you know him, Mrs Flanagan?"

She seemed not to have heard him. She was in her own world now. "He was a charmer. One evening I was walking home from school with a bunch of my friends and he pulled up alongside us. I can't remember what kind of car it was now. It was a flash little yoke. A sports car. Well I thought he was the bee's knees. So did all the girls. But he wanted to talk to me. Just me. Asked me if I wanted to go for a spin.

"Well of course I did. I hoped in and waved at the girls, delighted with myself. And that was it really. From then on, I was his girl. Went out for the best part of a year, we did."

"What happened? Why'd you break it off?"

"Oh I didn't," she said, smiling almost girlishly. "I wouldn't have done that. Not straight away anyway. I was stone mad about the fella. It was the legal system that separated us. He was caught for robbing a warehouse. He got sent to jail for four years."

"But..." Fiona glanced at Garda Conway who didn't try to stop her. "It seems like you didn't like him very much. So you're saying things ended well between you?"

The woman shook her head. "I wouldn't say that, no. It was alright at first. I suppose it seemed very romantic to an impressionable young one. Visiting the big tough boyfriend in jail. But time passed. I'd dropped out of school before he got sent to prison. I was starting to see the light on that. I went back. Started studying for my leaving. Fell in with a better crowd than I'd been hanging around with before. My old friends were all in couples, see. It soon got boring for them hanging around with a girl on her own pining for a fella on the inside. It was the best thing that ever happened to me. I finished school. Did a course. Eventually got a scholarship to college. I was flying it." Her expression grew serious. "And then of course *he* gets out. And it wasn't the same for him. If anything, he'd gotten worse when he was in there. He made a lot of connections in there. My God, did he think he was the tough man."

Fi winced. It was clear from Mrs Flanagan's face that what she was about to say next wasn't going to be easy to take. Her face was contorted with pain even thinking about it decades later.

"Yeah. You called it. He came for me. God, I don't even think he was that interested in me anymore, but it was the ego you see. He couldn't stand the idea that it was me who'd left *him*. He came to my mother's. I was still living there, of course telling everyone in college I lived in a flatshare in the inner city. He wouldn't listen. Banged on the doors and screamed until I came out."

"What happened then?" Fi was bewitched; filled with dread. This wasn't going to be some great romance with a happy ending.

Mrs Flanagan didn't answer. She looked up at them both and then slowly began rolling back her sleeve. For one awful moment, Fi thought she had a weapon up there; that she'd lulled them into silence to distract them and create an opportunity to pounce.

But there was no weapon. Fi gasped when she saw the woman's forearm. It didn't look like it belonged on a woman like Mrs Flanagan. She was well-to-do. Pristine. Socially connected.

She didn't look like the kind of woman to have an ugly knot of scars on her arm, ridged and red as if they'd only been made recently and not more than twenty years before.

A smile traced her face and flickered away again just as quickly as it had appeared. "It was a long time ago. I thought the wounds were healed. The physical ones certainly have—as much as they're ever going to, at least. But the mental ones..." she shook her head. "That surprised me. And now you can see why I reacted the way I did."

"What happened?"

There was a flicker of the more familiar Mrs Flanagan; the formidable middle-aged, upper middle-class society woman. "Oh come on now. Must I spell it out?"

"No," Fi coughed. "No. I'm sorry. I'm shocked, that's all. I never expected..."

"Not many do. I must admit that there aren't

many people who know the full story. Perhaps that was a mistake, but it's not one I wish to revisit now." She leaned forward so she was a fraction closer to them. "You know, most people thought I was some gold digger after Fintan's money. A lot of people still think it, especially when those inevitable articles crop up in the society pages talking about my quote-unquote humble beginnings."

"I imagine it must be tough."

"Oh come on now. You're not going to start mollycoddling me are you?"

Fi said nothing.

Mrs Flanagan's voice softened. "It was nothing to do with his money. We had friends in common in college. I was a shell after the attack. This whole new life I'd built up for myself was in tatters. It didn't matter that they'd shoved Pa in jail again. I felt as if he was always looming over me. My friends didn't really question why I turned into a silent ghost. They might have assumed it was the pressure of exams and that. But Fintan did. He showed an interest. He was so kind and gentle. He knew something was wrong. And one day I worked up the courage to show him my arm and my leg. The leg is much the same as what you saw—there's no need for me to show you. Anyway, they were still wrapped up in bandages. I thought he'd be disgusted, but he wasn't. Fintan is a good man. When he proposed..." she sighed. "I in no way want to play down my feelings for him, by the way. I loved him, but I also saw it as a chance to escape. Pa would never find me in Fintan's world. I wouldn't be Sharon Casey anymore. I'd be Mrs Fintan Flanagan. Untouchable." She shrugged. "Until now I suppose."

"He's dead."

"Sure he is," she said morosely. "But you lot turned up at my door today thinking I was involved in his murder. It's like he's taunting me from beyond the grave. Will I ever be rid of him?"

Garda Conway got to his feet. "I think we've taken up enough of your time. Your daughter will vouch for your whereabouts at the time of the murder?"

"Yes. The party was in full swing when we left. We could hear it through the door. I just wanted to get out of that town as soon as I recovered enough to remember what had happened." She reached her hand out for his. "Please. You mustn't tell anyone. I don't want people reading about this in the paper. It's the last thing my husband needs right now."

"Not if we have anything to do with it."

"Someone will leak it, I'm sure. There's no need to lie to me."

"We're not," Fi said, jumping to her feet too. "Nobody knows we came here. There's no official Garda record. My sister and I were planning to go to the Garda station this morning to tell them you were there. She had already left the house before I woke up so I panicked and figured she'd come here."

"Yes," Mrs Flanagan said nodding. "She did. I was just starting to tell her the real story when you burst in."

"She was comforting you when we arrived."

"Yes, she was. I think you shocked her almost as much as you shocked me."

"She'll be fine. We'll get going now. I'm truly sorry for the intrusion."

"Not at all. I suppose it's too optimistic to think that this'll be the last of my involvement in the investigation? All I ask is that you use discretion. Some of the things I told you are known by nobody except for my husband and mother. I'd prefer to keep it that way. It could be damaging to his career."

Fi glanced at Garda Conway, who shook his head. "Mrs Flanagan, this encounter never happened. We'll find another way to tie Mr

Kilcomer to his criminal past. You don't have to worry."

She shook her head. "Thank you. But it does concern me that you didn't know about it. He's been in jail on numerous occasions. It's not as if he's using a particularly cryptic alias. Why wasn't the connection made before?"

Garda Conway's expression darkened. "Believe me, that's something I'd very much like to know the answer to myself."

20

"Did you mean that?" Fi asked when they were back on the road. "All that about not knowing why his past didn't crop up in your investigation before now?"

Garda Conway nodded. "Sadly, I meant every word of it. It makes no sense at all."

"She said his name was slightly different. Pa then, Paddy now. I suppose it's a common enough name. Could your system have missed the connection?"

"Unlikely," he said after thinking about it for a moment. "The first name certainly, but not Kilcomer. But maybe you're right."

"What a piece of work all the same," Colm said after they'd told him the story. "Sounds like he got what was coming to him in the end."

Fi shuddered. She wouldn't wish such a fate on anyone, but she couldn't help agreeing with her brother's sentiment.

"So much for being a famous singer," she said, remembering something. "That's why they made such a fuss about that confidentiality agreement. Do you remember Kate?" She turned to Garda Conway. "Kate had to fill in a confidentiality agreement promising not to reveal any of the details of the wedding or attendees to anyone."

"That's not standard practice?"

"No. I mean, it sounds as if celebrities do it. I suppose it was part of the story that he was a singer once upon a time. It was a good cover story too."

"I suppose it meant you couldn't tell the press if you did happen to find out who he was."

"Yeah." She stared out the window, not envying Garda Conway's task in the slightest. "I guess this means you're going to have to go back to his family and try to get the truth from them."

"Maybe they didn't know."

"They must have. Why would they have used that confidentiality agreement otherwise? Why the lies about the showband?"

THE DRIVE back to Ballycashel felt like it took forever, even though the roads were relatively clear in the middle of the day when people were at work or at school. A dark cloud of frustration hung over them and they drove most of the way in silence. When they reached the service station, the three McCabes got out of the car and got into Marty's. Garda Conway raced on ahead. When they had asked what he was going to say to the sergeant, he just shrugged very calmly and said he'd think of something if Brennan asked. There was always someone wanting help with non-urgent problems in town and Sergeant Brennan was very clear that he didn't want any involvement in such trivial cases.

Within a matter of seconds, Garda Conway's car had disappeared off into the distance. Colm maintained a steady speed of 120 kilometres an hour now that the pressure was off them. It wasn't in his nature to abide by the rules so strictly, but the station wagon was almost old enough to be considered a classic car (without the inflated value, of course) so it was unwise to try and push it if it wasn't necessary.

Fi sighed in the front seat. "I feel like we're even further away from solving this than we were this morning."

Colm glanced at her, his face puzzled. "So? We've

confirmed your woman had nothing to do with it. It's up to the guards now."

Fi thought about it and was inclined to agree. Surprisingly, it was Kate who piped up from the back seat before she could answer.

"That all depends," she said, sounding miserable. "The next wedding is more important than ever now that the Flanagans want to cancel."

Fi spun around, almost giving herself whiplash in the process. "They're still talking about cancelling? You couldn't manage to convince them?"

"No," Kate said shaking her head. "We were talking about it when you burst in all GI Jane. Mrs Flanagan is terrified to have her name associated with Ballycashel. If Mr Flanagan goes there, it's bound to make the society pages. She's worried that there might be a mention of the murder. Seeing her name and Kilcomer's name in the same article just seems like too much for her."

Fi shook her head. That changed things. That changed things a lot. "So if the guards aren't out of the pub by next week...?"

Kate shook her head. Her siblings had never seen her look so frazzled before. As one of the youngest in the family, she'd always had someone on hand to bail her out of any troublesome situations before they became too serious.

"I'll be ruined. All the profit from the first two weddings will be wiped out. I took out a loan to pay for all the supplies. The first payment's going to be due next month. The money I made off the first two weddings will cover some of the payments, but not all of them."

Fi winced. "What if you structure it so you pay off the bank loan first and then worry about the money you owe to us? We're family. We can be flexible."

"I've already done that," Kate said, worrying at her nails. "I made some mistakes with the first wedding. I paid more for things than I should have and the profits reflect that."

"Is there anything we can do?"

"Yeah. You can help me find out who did this so we can move ahead with the next wedding and then pray I can find a booking to replace the Flanagans."

"That's a big ask," Colm said laughing. It was obvious he was only trying to lighten the mood but Kate didn't see the funny side.

"Yeah it is, Col. But it's my only option. If I don't pay back that loan…"

"You'll pay it back," Fi said decisively. "I'm sure Garda Conway is making progress already."

HE WASN'T, as it turned out. Fi didn't dare go visit him at the Garda station for fear of raising Brennan's suspicions about what he'd been doing all morning and afternoon. But he had promised he'd let them know if there was an update. So far, she'd received no word from him and it was almost eight at night.

"At least ye followed up that clue," Margaret said, as she brought out a big pot of stew. "Even if it did turn out to be a dead end."

"Really? It led to nothing. We're lost now. We've heard nothing from Garda Conway. The guards are probably as lost as we are. Useless shower."

Fi looked up at her sister, unused to hearing such defeat in her voice. "We're not lost. We found out the man's true identity. And look here." She handed her sister her phone, which she'd been quietly focused on for the past several minutes. "I've found several articles about him. My search turned up nothing before and I assumed that was just because maybe there wasn't just a great internet record of showband singers. But plugging in crime, drugs and gang?

There's articles about him as recently as five years ago. He seems to have put his head down since then but maybe that means he started feeling pressure from rivals or whatever. I doubt he was after going and turning his life around."

"So? That tells us nothing. We still don't know who the killer is."

"That's true," Fi mused. "But look at it this way. We can do our own investigation. We can find photos of all of his associates and enemies and see if we recognise any of them from the day of the wedding."

"What does that prove?"

"Nothing. But it's a start. And it gives us something to work with. We'll try and write a list of anyone around here with a grudge against him. Anyone who moved here recently or was the victim of his gang. We wouldn't be able to do that on our own, of course, but we can start."

"What are you saying? That a local was involved?"

Fi shrugged. "It seems a bit more likely now we're dealing with a gangland figure and not some singer from the seventies. Chances are he's ruined a lot of lives. Look at Mrs Flanagan. He didn't ruin her, but we saw how she reacted to him."

Kate nodded slowly. "So you think someone saw him and realised who he was? Then they killed him on the spur of the moment?"

"Maybe." Fi bit her lip. It felt like the field had been thrown wide open. There was something she wasn't factoring in, but she couldn't figure out what it was.

"I'll check the cameras tomorrow. The guards were looking for a guest. It was less important when we thought it might be Mrs Flanagan because she wouldn't have been caught on camera. What if..."

"But Fi! Surely the guards are all over this!"

She shrugged. "It doesn't seem that way, does it?"

21

Garda Conway called round to the house early the following morning not long after they'd gotten up. He looked sheepish when he saw they were still in their dressing gowns.

"Sorry for the early visit. I wanted to call over before Brennan came into the station." He rummaged in his pocket and pulled out a wrinkled sheaf of pages. "I have good and bad news. The good news is it was easy to come up with a list of known associates. The bad news is there's not been much activity in those quarters lately." He handed Fi the bundle of pages.

She took it and skimmed through the list, looking for familiar faces. "This guy!" she said, pointing at the fifth picture down. "He looks familiar."

Garda Conway cleared his throat. "Look at the name."

"Oh." He had the same surname as the victim.

"His brother. By all accounts they've been as thick as thieves—and I've never heard that phrase used in such an appropriate way. But he wasn't at the wedding as it happens. He's currently serving time. I imagine you're thinking of Paddy."

She shook her head and looked through the other photos, turning the page and doing the same on the next page and the next. There were no other familiar faces.

"So there's nothing then?"

He shook his head. "Not in terms of his associates. Like I say, it's been quiet. No reports of feuds or other troubles. Now, I have a list here of a different kind. These are members of other gangs. Known enemies of Kilcomer."

Fiona took the second set of pages a lot more enthusiastically. She felt certain that these ones held the link, though she couldn't remember any strange men coming into the pub during the function.

She scanned the photos carefully, imagining the men with different hairstyles or in more formal clothing than the tracksuits most were wearing in the pictures. Even focussing all her attention on each one yielded nothing.

Disappointed, she handed back the list. "Sorry. None of them look familiar. I guess that's the bad news."

"No, the bad news is the other thing I've to tell you. We've run background checks on all of the attendees. On first glance, none of them had a grudge."

"None of them were involved with gangs?"

He shook his head. "No."

"So who did this? And why didn't you pick up the gang connection immediately? Surely it's all over his record in your system."

"I don't know, Fiona," he said gravely. "You have to remember that murders aren't all that common around here. And we had a lot of people to speak to. It might have been overlooked."

"It seems like a big thing to overlook."

"What can I tell you? This isn't like those other murders. The victim's not a local. It's not as easy to track down his associates. The feeling is that this is a gang thing. Someone snuck in. It's just unfortunate that the camera didn't manage to catch whoever it was. But we'll find them." He didn't sound very optimistic.

Fiona frowned. Something about this wasn't right, but she couldn't put her finger on what it was.

He sighed. "It's an awful mess. I'm sure they chose Ballycashel to keep things simple; to avoid any press coverage. And now look what happened."

"So his daughter knew?"

He shrugged. "We haven't followed up that line of enquiry with them. We spoke to her before we knew the truth."

"I'm surprised you're even investigating this at all. Isn't there an organised crime unit to deal with this sort of thing?"

"I suppose Brennan thought it'd be an easy solve; a feather in his cap. Now we all have to pay the price for that." He smiled. "I suppose I shouldn't complain when there's all that lovely overtime to think about."

She laughed, but there was no enthusiasm in it. Her problem remained.

"How long do you think it's going to take for you to finish up at the pub?"

He shook his head. "I couldn't say. If you want my honest opinion, I don't know what we're still doing in there. But that's just between you and me."

"What are you saying?"

"I think you know."

She had her suspicions, but it seemed beyond

believable that a grown man would be capable of such a thing. "Do you honestly think Brennan is stalling just to annoy us?"

He shrugged. "I'd never suggest such a thing publicly. But I can see no other reason for us still being in there. If there was anything to be found we would have found it by now."

22

With the pub off limits and her internet searches not turning up anything, the only thing Fiona could do was look at the video footage from the pub on the day of the wedding.

She borrowed Kate's laptop and logged in to her account purely because she couldn't think of anything else useful to do and she was getting fed up of loitering around her parents' house. Kate was in an utterly foul mood as the penalty fees from the hired crockery and glassware continued to mount. She'd rather watch grainy black and white footage than listen to another minute of Kate huffing.

It didn't help that she didn't have her own space in the house. There was always the option to stay with Kate rather than on the couch, but the couch was preferable even if it meant being forced to witness Ben's PlayStation marathons when she wanted to sleep.

In the middle of the day on a weekday, though, the sitting room was blissfully empty. She settled down on the recliner chair and brought up the video footage from the morning of the wedding. She already knew it wouldn't show the entire wedding party.

On the screen, there were no guests present yet. It was still too early. Occasionally she and Kate came into view at the very edge of the screen, bustling around setting up the tables and centrepieces. There was her mother. Jason came around from behind the bar and began to set up a triangle of wine glasses. Then champagne flutes. She watched as a black and white version of herself came and spoke to him.

She looked cheerful. Stressed but happy.

Jason, on the other hand, seemed off somehow. It was there in his body language. She hadn't noticed it at the time—she'd been too busy and preoccupied— but it was clear now. He looked like a man who didn't want to be part of the conversation.

Sure enough, when she left him a moment or so later, he visibly relaxed. She focussed on him for a while, carefully placing the glasses and standing back every so often to check the layout.

How well did she know him? Not very. Kate had taken him on when the Kilcomers asked for enough staff to be on hand so that their guests would be treated to a luxurious experience. In Kate's mind, that had translated to cocktails and expensive spirits, and she had suspected Fi wouldn't be able to handle fifty cocktail orders all on her own.

She frowned. But what exactly did she have to go off? So what if Jason hadn't felt like chatting with her that day?

She sighed and unpaused the footage. Her eyes started to glaze after another twenty minutes of watching herself hurry across the screen. She sped it up. Kate left to go back to the church.

Fi smiled as Angus entered the bar a little while later. She watched herself hurry over to him and chat for a few moments. They stood by the door. She remembered that part. She was coaching him through what Kate wanted him to do: stand and greet people, taking their coats if they wanted.

Nothing happened for a while. Fi and Angus were still by the door. Tom came out from behind the bar with a crate of glasses. He cast a quick look at Fi and Angus over by the door. When he turned back towards the bar—towards the camera—he scowled and shook his head.

Fi gasped and rewound the footage. She played it back at normal speed. This time, Tom's strange reaction was even more pronounced. He looked absolutely disgusted. There was no obvious reason why —it wasn't as if Fi and Angus were being particularly clingy.

But again, that told her nothing except that perhaps she was fundamentally unlikeable by bar staff.

She forwarded it on. The Flanagans arrived. Then the guests. Finally the family. She leaned closer and alternated between watching them and watching Mrs Flanagan.

There was nothing. She held her breath as the family moved further into the bar after taking glasses of champagne from the tray Fi had been holding.

It was only a split second view, but it was enough to back up Mrs Flanagan's story. As soon as Paddy Kilcomer passed the snug where she was sitting, her mouth flew open in a horrified grimace. A moment later, she was collapsed on the table and her daughter was moving closer to her, frantically looking around for help. There was no sound on the tape, but Fi remembered the strange noise she'd made. She'd heard it because of where she'd been standing. Sure enough, she watched herself hurry over, with Kate arriving a moment later.

She took a breath and composed herself. So far, she'd learned nothing new from watching the tape. And the clock was ticking.

Finbarr arrived. He lifted Mrs Flanagan out of the booth and carried her carefully out of shot.

Then everything quietened down as the guests took their seats for the meal. It was mainly staff that bustled past the camera from that point. A few guests came to the bar to get drinks, but the victim wasn't one of them.

And that was it. Somewhere to the left of the edge of the shot, a man was murdered. There was no indication of it on screen. In fact, the only reason she knew it had happened was a crowd of distraught-looking guests suddenly hurried to the bar.

Then the paramedics arrived. She watched them stop, get directions to the casualty and then hurry through the bar.

Fiona shook her head. What did the video mean? Maybe she should take stills and send them to Conway. One of the guests who ordered a drink at the bar could have spiked it with something and given it to the father of the bride and nobody would have been any the wiser.

She was still mulling this over a moment later when Brennan appeared. He hurried straight into the pub without pausing, eyes focused straight ahead. He disappeared from view just as quickly as he'd appeared.

Fi frowned and rewound back to just before Brennan entered. This time, she played it slower than real time and watched the screen carefully.

Yes. She hadn't been sure the first time she'd seen it, but now she had no doubt. Brennan had known where to go.

How did that work?

She paused the footage and thought about it. Brennan came into the pub and whoever was behind the bar could have pointed to the back where everything was happening.

That could work, she thought. But she was still unsettled. Unsettled enough to watch it again and again.

Something else struck her. She went back and watched the paramedics' entrance. They were hesitant, bursting in but then slowing to figure out what was going on and who needed their assistance.

Brennan hadn't.

Not only that, but she remembered something else. She'd been behind the bar when he came in.

And far from telling him where to go, she'd tried to hold him back.

She watched Brennan's entrance once more and stopped the footage.

Crazy theories were spinning around in her head. She had to get out.

23

She went to see Garda Conway on the pretext of asking some questions about her application for a PI licence. As soon as the sergeant heard what she was there for, his lip curled in disgust. He stalked off soon after that, leaving them alone at the desk.

"Any advances?"

"No," Garda Conway murmured. "We think a criminal associate snuck in."

"Unnoticed by fifty people and staff?"

He shrugged. "I don't know. Maybe he passed himself off as staff."

"But that's crazy! That's like something out of a movie."

"I don't know, Fiona," he muttered. "Don't shoot the messenger."

She tried not to let her exasperation get the

better of her. She had to solve this thing—it seemed like she was the only one who wanted to. But it was hard. She rolled her eyes. "I'm surprised he's not trying to blame me for it the way he's blocking me out of my pub."

"Oh no. He says this is a Dublin problem and how could we think of bringing the innocent people of Ballycashel into it."

Fi made a face. "He's changed his tune a lot in the last few months. He couldn't wait to throw people in the cells before."

"I know. It's not like him."

Fiona took a deep breath and exhaled slowly. Nothing was going to be gained from slagging Brennan. She leaned closer to the desk so she wouldn't have to raise her voice louder than a whisper. "Brennan made it to the scene very early."

Garda Conway looked at her levelly. "I told you before, I'm sure. We can see the emergency callouts in our system."

"Can you see it there? Right in front of you?"

"Of course. It's all linked up to the system."

"What did it say?"

He tapped at the keyboard for several seconds. "Here it is, yes." He paused for a few moments, eyes moving across the screen. "Male. Fifties. Collapsed, suspected dead in McCabe's pub Ballycashel."

"So," Fiona said, biting her lip. "How did Brennan know it was a murder? How could he have been sure from that report?"

Garda Conway turned away from the screen and looked at her directly. "I imagine it was to do with where the ambulance was called to. My guess is he saw *McCabe's* and he saw it as a possible excuse to harass you." He glanced over his shoulder. "Off the record, of course."

"I understand." She was disappointed. She'd expected him to agree; to tell her it was weird that Brennan had decided to investigate what was likely to be natural causes even though he usually preferred to leave anything trivial to the other Gardaí.

But she knew Garda Conway was right. His interest was probably more to do with the fact that it had taken place at her pub than anything else.

Maybe it had been a slow day at the office for Brennan. Either way, he'd hit the jackpot: her pub had been closed for four days now and there was no sign of it being returned to her any time soon.

"It's so frustrating! Why can't he just release the

pub back to me? What good is it doing him to keep it closed?"

Garda Conway smiled sympathetically. "You know, he's got a call booked in half an hour. He was bragging about it earlier—God knows why. I'd say you're safe going in there to get some of your things."

Fiona beamed at him. "Thank you," she whispered, before walking out as quickly as she could without raising Brennan's suspicions should he decide to look out of his office.

SHE WAS VERY careful not to disturb the crime scene tape as she let herself into the pub. She expected to encounter Garda Fitzpatrick or some members of the technical crew, but there was nobody there. She looked around. It felt like months had passed since the day of the wedding, even though it was only a matter of days.

Her eyes fell on the kitchen door and she took a couple of steps towards it before stopping herself. It would be very obvious if the place was suddenly cleaned up when she wasn't supposed to be in there. She turned away. No matter how much she wanted to get the place back to normal, she knew she had to wait.

She had intended to quickly check on the bar before hurrying upstairs to get some clothes. She found herself lingering at the bar instead.

She stared at the wall opposite. Brennan should have been the last person on her mind, but she couldn't help picturing his mad dash through the pub. What was wrong with that picture? There was something, and it had been bothering her ever since she saw the tape.

She moved behind the bar and picked up a cloth that had been left untidily strewn on the counter. She wrung it in her hands, pretending she was cleaning a glass or wiping down the counter.

She traced her eyes along the wall, recalling how his focus had been directly ahead. Someone might have pointed towards the back, but he wouldn't have seen them. Not facing the way he had been.

She frowned.

Even if someone had called to him—which she couldn't remember happening—it would have taken a few seconds for him to react. But he hadn't. He'd gone straight there.

She rolled her eyes. He must have seen the paramedics—he must have—because he didn't need to be told where they were and what was going on. Even the paramedics had been unsure when they first entered. That was why his reaction had confused her. It was a pub, after all, and didn't all of the action usually take place at or very close to the bar? But several large men in bright high-vis clothing would have been hard to miss.

She moved out from behind the bar and walked to the door. She'd stood in this exact place on thousands of occasions during her life, but she'd never really paid attention. It was always just the pub. Her parents' pub when she was a child, the empty pub when it closed down, her bar when she decided to lease it from them and reopen it.

It really was time to get going. If Brennan caught her lingering in there he was bound to cause trouble for her. And it seemed obvious to her that her imagination was running away. There was no big puzzle in Brennan's actions on the day of the murder.

She pivoted around and looked back towards the area where the tables were still set up and abandoned.

She frowned and her heart began to hammer. The huge room itself was rectangular, but thanks to the way it was fitted out, it was more like a series of nooks and crannies joined by a narrow central pathway. And standing at the door where she was, she realised that Brennan couldn't have seen the paramedics at work. Because the table Kilcomer had been sitting at—the area where Finbarr had eased him to the floor and began treatment—was completely blocked from view. She walked briskly in that direction, just as Brennan had done.

It was only when she got past the bar that she saw the table and the far side of it where they'd laid him out and tried to resuscitate him in some semblance of privacy.

But before Brennan had gotten that far, Fiona had intervened and tried to stop him. Yes, she remembered stepping in front of him and trying to stall him. And even then, he had known exactly where he was going.

24

Fiona's mind was racing when she got back to her parents' house. She couldn't work out what her recent discovery meant. She'd mulled it over all the way back home, thinking of more and more ludicrous ways of finding out the truth.

Like maybe someone else had shouted to Brennan and he'd heard them but not acknowledged them. But who had reaction times like that?

No, this had to mean something. But what? For all of Brennan's weirdness, she'd seen him enter the pub. It had been after the paramedics had arrived. He'd arrived after the murder.

So what did it mean?

As soon as she got in the door, Kate launched herself at her and tried to corral her into helping with the preparations for the Flanagan wedding.

Kate had finally managed to convince Marie to keep her on as the wedding planner, but the Flanagans wouldn't budge on the venue. It had to be someplace different.

Fiona thought taking her mind off the case might help, but it was obvious after less than half an hour that she could think of little else.

It all circulated in her mind, infuriatingly out of reach.

"Come on, Fi," her sister complained. "You're not focusing."

"Yeah I am. I'm thinking."

"I don't need you to think. I need you to search for a venue that's not too far from here with space for a wedding at short notice."

Fi jumped off her chair, hurried through the kitchen and out the back door. It was cold, but it didn't matter.

She needed to think.

She wished she'd brought a notebook with her. Maybe that would help her get her thoughts in order. She turned to go back into the kitchen and got a fright when she found her mother and sister watching her from the large window. She wasn't exactly surprised though.

She ducked in, holding her hands up in self-defence. "I don't have time for this right now. I need to think."

"Oh, you need to think? Well, how about—"

She grabbed the flour-covered old notebook her mother used for recipes and was gone before Kate could finish her sentence.

She sat back down under the kitchen windowsill. It wasn't particularly comfortable there and it was a bit too close to the drain for her liking, but it was the only place in the garden that couldn't be seen from the window right above her.

That suited her fine.

FI STARED at the list she'd scrawled on the page. It had taken her the best part of half an hour and she was hungry and cold. And she'd gotten nowhere. She bit her lip and read over the points again.

- *Brennan knew where the victim was.*
- *Couldn't have seen paramedics.*
- *Didn't know it was a murder beforehand*

>>*would he really have gone to all that trouble for a grudge against me/family?*

- *Suspects always non-locals. Not like him.*
- *Man was poisoned. Doesn't sound very... mob.*
- *We didn't see anyone else come in during the day. None of us did. Me, Kate, Mam, Dad, Granny...*

She scratched her head and read through it once more. It wasn't like she needed to. Her list was so incomplete and short that she already knew it from memory.

She was impatient now. Impatient and hungry. She thought hard. What action could she take from that list? There didn't seem to be much. She couldn't exactly go and confront Brennan. What would he do only deny everything? And he'd probably have her sent to a mental hospital for good measure. It'd be just like him...

Her eyes widened. They'd been saying for days how strange it was that he wasn't trying to pin the murder on a local. Of course, that could be because none of the locals were suspicious.

She smiled and jumped to her feet.

She knew how to find out one way or the other.

FIONA FORCED a smile onto her face. It was hard. Being in the same room as Brennan usually made her want to throw up, but she had no choice. Not if she wanted to progress this thing and find out what was going on.

"So," he said, looking about as pleased about her visit as she was to be there. "You say you have information about this case."

She nodded. "Yes. I think I do."

"And why is it you haven't shared this with us before?"

"I didn't think it was important. I didn't really think about it until now."

"I see. And how am I to know this isn't some misguided attempt to get your pub back?"

"You'll see if you look into what I'm about to tell you, I suppose. Won't it be obvious if there's a genuine lead in there? I mean, you're the police officer."

His eyes narrowed and she reminded herself that this was no time for petty points scoring. She needed him onside and she needed him to listen to her.

"Look, I think there's something here. On the day of the wedding, I saw Mrs Davis close to the top table. She was staring at Mr Kilcomer and she did *not* look happy to see him."

He shrugged. "So? That doesn't necessarily mean anything."

"Well, have you looked into any possible links to her? What if she knew him before?"

"What do you mean, knew him before? Before what?"

She certainly wasn't going to bring Mrs Flanagan's name into it, so she thought for a moment. "Before. Like in a past life. What if they had a relationship years ago or something?"

Brennan flushed as if she'd slapped him. "Then I'm sure, Miss McCabe, that she would have told me about it."

"You spoke to her?"

He nodded as if he resented the fact that he was even answering her. "Just like I spoke to everyone who was there that day. Yourself included."

She thought back. She had spoken to Brennan briefly, worried he was going to try and blame everything on her. He hadn't, in fact. He had seemed completely disinterested and had barely asked her anything. She'd been relieved at the time, but now it was puzzling.

"You quizzed her about her links to Kilcomer?"

He pursed his lips. "I interrogated her thoroughly, Miss McCabe. Not that this is any of your business."

Fiona baulked. She'd heard a very different story from Mrs Davis. "So you'll look into this? I think it could be important. You should have seen the look on her face. I'm telling you." Fiona swallowed and sent a silent apology to Mrs Davis for any harassment she was about to bring on the woman. "Her fists were so tight her knuckles were white and it was almost like she was snarling at him. I was so scared looking at her that I think I blocked it from my mind."

"Did you now?" he said with undisguised loathing. "Well your feelings have nothing to do with my investigation. So I'd thank you to keep your nose out of this."

"I'm only trying to tell you something that might be important."

He just stared at her as if he despised her more than anyone in the world. Eventually she got up and left.

IT WAS a long wait until that evening but she didn't want to risk trying to make contact with Garda

Conway any sooner. As it was, she was pushing it a little bit by going to Phelan's to see him after doing the same thing so recently.

But she had to. She had to know.

She followed the familiar routine of entering the pub, chatting with the old men around the bar and then casually making her way to Garda Conway. This time, she fed them some nonsense about finding a key on the floor of the pub and wondering if it was something to do with the crime. There was no fear of any of them passing it on to Brennan— none of them could stand the sight of him.

"Garda Conway," she whispered, sitting down in the booth opposite him.

"Fiona." He jerked his head upward in greeting. "You're here about the matter we discussed this morning, I take it."

She'd pretended to drop her bag on the way out of the station after she'd been to see the sergeant. Out of sight of the sergeant's office of course. She'd used the opportunity to tell Garda Conway what she'd told the sergeant.

"I am."

He took a sip of his pint and looked at her seriously. "Brennan is handling the investigation himself so I have to be very careful about checking the files.

He's very protective of it. I don't want him thinking I'm meddling in his case."

"So you couldn't see?"

"No," he said with a small smile. "That's not what I said at all. But I had to be quick about it."

Fiona's heart leapt. This was it. The strange niggle that had been bothering her for days was about to be either confirmed or shown to be nothing more than a foolish theory. She tried to figure out which one it was from Garda Conway's expression, but it told her nothing.

"Well?"

He shook his head. "Nothing."

"What do you mean?" she asked too quickly. "My suspicions were unfounded or you found nothing in there?"

"Your suspicions?"

She nodded, realising that she'd had to leave a lot out that morning. "I really hammed it up in there. I talked about Mrs Davis like she was a crazed killer. He told me he interrogated her thoroughly on the day of the murder, but that's not what she told me. So what did his notes say about my visit?"

Garda Conway shook his head. "There was no record of your visit in our system. And he hasn't reached out to Mrs Davis for further questioning."

She bit her lip. Her crazy theory suddenly seemed less like a conspiracy and more like a possible explanation. Now that her point had been proven, she was suddenly filled with doubt. "Maybe it's because he thinks I'm just trying to get my pub back. What does this prove anyway?"

But Garda Conway didn't leap to accept that justification. He sighed. "Even if he did think you were a crackpot, that still doesn't explain it."

"Meaning?"

"Meaning he logs everything in the file. Usually. You should have seen the file he had on Hanlon, and that was for an unpaid television licence for God's sake."

"So you think I'm on to something here?"

He shrugged. "Maybe, but it still doesn't get us anywhere. All I can tell you is it's very odd that he didn't make a record of your visit. I've seen his notes. He wouldn't have held back on being very dismissive in his report, but it's very strange that he hasn't made one at all."

"Okay, so where does that leave us? What do we do now?"

He smiled sadly. "We don't have the slightest notion what's going on, other than that the Garda Commissioner's friend's son isn't as thorough as he usually is. I can't exactly take that to internal affairs now, can I? We've got nothing more to go on than the fact that Brennan didn't file your statement. He'll explain that away easily. He'll claim he's made his home in Ballycashel and knows the people here. No one has a motive. It's an outsider."

"But why's he so convinced? He'll usually stop at nothing to point the finger at a resident of this town."

"Beats me," Garda Conway said with a heavy sigh.

"Okay, so we're still in the same position. Brennan's refusing to blame this on a local. He didn't question any of us too rigorously and he won't even look into Mrs Davis even though I told him all sorts of tales about her." She shook her head. "What does that tell us? It has to tell us something, right?"

He narrowed his eyes. "It tells us," he said, taking a long slug of his pint. "That Brennan's connected to this in some way. That's all I know. Now, I can only think of one way for us to find out any more about what's going on, but it's not going to be pleasant. Do you hear me?"

She nodded eagerly, pulse buzzing in her temples.

"Okay," he said gruffly. "I'll pick you up at your

house tomorrow morning at seven. None of this meeting on the motorway nonsense. But you have to promise me one thing."

"What?"

"That you'll do whatever I tell you. Believe me, it's for your own protection."

25

Fiona shivered as they stopped at a checkpoint and Garda Roche stuck his head out to speak to the uniformed man in the little office alongside him. She'd barely slept the night before wondering where they were off to the next day.

She could never have imagined it'd be a prison.

Once they'd parked up and entered the building, it almost reminded her of going to the airport. Except there was to be no fun holiday at the end of this.

"Why are we here?" she whispered, after being patted down by a very serious-looking female officer.

"Shh," Garda Conway said, gesturing ahead. "Not a word. I'm not sure I should have even brought you here."

Fiona shivered and fell silent as they were led

through a corridor that smelled strongly of cleaning products. Her curiosity grew stronger as they were led into a room with a row of kiosk-like spaces with chairs on either side of a glass barrier in the middle.

"Wait," Garda Conway said sharply. He stopped abruptly and ushered Fiona back out of the room. "This was a terrible idea. I'll get you to wait in the waiting room if that's okay."

She shook her head. "No, it's fine. Honestly. I want to help."

"You can help by waiting in the waiting room. No arguing." He walked her back there and left without another word.

Fiona was left in a stuffy room that did everything it could to seem cheery but still came across pretty grim. There was a low table in the middle of the room stacked with dog-eared magazines. Shelves in the corner contained toys and books for kids. She'd never been in a prison before. She'd joked about it, of course, but being in there for real freaked her out more than she could ever have imagined.

She began to wonder if it was wise to pursue this Brennan thing. Could he have her sent to a place like this; on the opposite side of the glass in that awful visiting room Conway had run her out of? She hoped not. What would be the point in getting her pub back if she was stuck behind bars and unable to run it?

Not for the first time, Fiona wondered what she was doing with her life. All this energy spent trying to run a pub that was still nowhere close to turning a meaningful profit.

She thought of her granny then and smiled. If she lived and worked in Dublin, there'd be no way she'd get to spend as much time with her family as she did.

That has to count for something, she thought.

She wasn't left mulling over her thoughts for very long. Garda Conway was back within ten minutes of leaving her, and he did not look happy.

"What is it? Did you find out what you needed? Who were you visiting anyway?"

He looked around cagily.

"Come on. There's nobody here to overhear."

But he wouldn't tell her anything until they'd left the building and returned to his squad car. It was only when they were both inside with their seatbelts on that he turned to her.

"Kilcomer's brother. He's some piece of work."

"Was he helpful?"

Garda Conway pursed his lips. "About as helpful as Brennan. I made it very clear that I was here about another matter and that I didn't care what he gets up to in his spare time. He wouldn't have a bar of it."

"I don't get it," Fi said. "He's in jail. How was he going to help?"

"I hoped he could tell us something that explains why Brennan's handling this differently to any other investigation. Like hell he'd help. He's one of those types who wouldn't help a Garda if his life depended on it."

She sighed. "Maybe you should have sent me in there."

He spluttered and jerked his head. "Good God no. No, Fiona. It was a mistake of me to even think of bringing you along to an interview with that gurrier."

She stared out the window as they manoeuvred out of the car park and back through the barrier. She was trying to imagine what Kilcomer's brother was like. How could he be so different to his brother? She hadn't had any dealings with Paddy, but he'd looked like a perfectly nice normal man in his fifties.

"How does a man change that much?" she asked when they'd finally gotten themselves back on the motorway.

Garda Conway glanced at her. Traffic was too

thick for him to really take his attention off the road. "You're asking about Kilcomer?" He sighed. "I don't know. I never met the man."

"He seemed nice. Just from looking at him. His nice suit. He looked friendly. Am I being naïve or is there something we're not seeing?"

He laughed gruffly. "You can dress a wolf up in a suit and he's still a wolf. But I don't know. Maybe the man did change."

"You don't sound very sure."

"Ah." He jerked his head backwards. "He'd be the first fella I ever knew to change if he did."

THE NEXT PLACE they pulled up at was intimidating too, but for entirely different reasons. It was a large detached Georgian house in a suburb south of the city and close to the sea.

"What's this place?" Fi asked. She couldn't for the life of her work out how a place like this could be relevant to their case.

Garda Conway just smiled at her. "Surprising, isn't it? I suppose ye wouldn't have known because the daughter lives in an apartment with her husband. Come on."

Frowning, she followed him up the stone driveway and stood to one side as he knocked on the door using the shiny brass knocker.

The door opened after a few moments and a familiar woman stood in the threshold.

Fi stared at her in disbelief for a few seconds before forcing a smile onto her face. She would never for a moment have imagined that this elegant place belonged to a criminal. Then again, she'd gleaned all of her knowledge about gang members from the TV.

"Mrs Kilcomer," Garda Conway said, clearing his throat. "I'm Garda Conway from Ballycashel. I won't take up too much of your time."

Her pleasant smile faltered for a moment before recovering. "Of course. Come in."

They stepped inside and she led them into the first room on the right. It was a similar setup to the Flanagans' living room in that it contained a lot of expensive, understated furniture, but this was on an even larger scale. It was all creams and subtle hints of golds. There wasn't an animal skin print or a purple item of furniture in sight. It was not the type of place she would have expected for a gangster's family.

"I had a few questions for you."

Mrs Kilcomer nodded briskly. "Of course. Yes. Anything."

"Let's start with your wedding guests. Is there any chance any of them could have been involved?"

"No," she said, shaking her head. "I've already told you this. No way."

Garda Conway cleared his throat. "Of course. But do you mind telling me how you can be so certain? If I understand it correctly, your husband was involved in some less-than-savoury activities."

She threw her head back and laughed—much to their surprise. "That's putting it mildly."

"So you don't think it's possible that one of your husband's old associates could have struck at the wedding?" He flushed. "My apologies for putting it in such a way."

She waved her hand to dismiss his concern. "I can put my hand on my heart and tell you that none of my husband's old cronies were at that wedding. I should know, I went through the list myself with a fine-tooth comb. When they first announced the engagement, Patrick said he'd throw a huge wedding party for his little princess. I was dead against it. I urged her to wait until he cooled off before she made any plans. It was I who insisted she go for a small place in the middle of nowhere. Not only that, but I told her to delay as long as possible before booking the thing and make sure she got a confidentiality agreement."

"Why?"

"You know why! Let's not beat around the bush, Garda. We both know what my husband used to be. He was a gangster, pure and simple. At least he was until I met him. We're safe here in the house. Outside it? All bets are off. Why do you think I chose a place in the middle of nowhere?"

Fi glanced at Garda Conway but said nothing.

"Until you met him? But I was on the understanding that he'd been involved in criminal activities until as recently as five years ago."

"He was. That's when I met him."

Fi frowned.

"I'm the girls' step-mother. Not their mother."

"I see," Garda Conway said.

"I told all this to the sergeant. It wasn't one of our guests. This was a gangland thing. Some old grudge. If I was you, I'd check the records and see which of Patrick's old enemies was recently released from jail."

"How can you be so sure, Mrs Kilcomer?"

"Why else?"

Conway cleared his throat. "Often it's a close relative or associate."

Her eyes bore into him. "What are you suggesting, Garda? That I or one of my step-daughters killed him for his money? Don't be absurd. Look around you. This is the house I grew up in. I'm not in need of money. I've just lost my husband."

"I'm sorry," he said soberly. "You asked about other motives and I mentioned a common one. I was in no way suggesting... Anyway. Do you have any idea which of his old enemies might have been capable of doing something like this?"

She sighed. "No. He was out of that life. I don't know any of those people."

"Is there a possibility he was up to his old tricks again, as it were?"

For the first time, Mrs Kilcomer became guarded. "What? No."

"It could be nothing. But maybe he tried to protect you from it. You were obviously brought up in a very different lifestyle to him."

"What are you trying to say?" she snapped.

Fi held her hands up, shocked at the woman's reaction. "Sometimes people hide things from their partners. That's all."

"Exactly. It wasn't a slight against your late husband, Mrs Kilcomer. Just an honest question."

Mrs Kilcomer sighed and collected herself, and Fiona reminded herself not to read too much into the woman's reactions. After all, she'd been witness to something no-one should ever have to see.

"No, I don't think he was hiding something from me. I'm a psychologist. I spent my whole career working with criminals. I know how they operate."

"Is that how you met?"

"I don't see how that's relevant."

"Of course. My apologies."

"No, no," Mrs Kilcomer said, rubbing her cheek. "It's fine. It's just that I had quite a hard time when we got first got together. I had to choose between him and my career. I chose him, obviously, and I did it without regrets." She smiled sadly. "But my colleagues weren't exactly impressed with my decision."

"I can imagine."

"Yes."

They lapsed into silence then, and as time passed it became increasingly obvious that Fi and Garda Conway weren't welcome anymore. Nor did they wish to impose for any longer than they needed to.

"One last question, Mrs Kilcomer," Garda Conway said, standing up. "Did you see anyone suspicious that day? It's difficult for us to imagine how somebody managed to get in and out unseen that day. Was there anyone who looked like they shouldn't have been there?"

She shook her head. "No. Patrick was no fool and I was with him all day. But that's these gangs for you. They're able to do things normal people like us can't. We thought we were protecting him by planning the wedding at the last minute and taking all these precautions, but that obviously wasn't enough. Somehow word got out."

"I'm sorry." Garda Conway nodded formally and headed for the door.

She stood to see them out, looking pale and drawn. Fiona felt guilty for having dragged her back through the events of that day.

"Thank you," she whispered, at a loss for anything else to say.

Mrs Kilcomer opened the front door and stood aside to let them exit.

"One last thing, Mrs Kilcomer," Garda Conway said briskly. "Did your husband have any links to Sergeant Brennan?"

Mrs Kilcomer turned as pale as the delicate

porcelain vase on the hall table behind her. Her fingers dug into the door.

"Mrs Kilcomer?"

She cleared her throat. "I'm sorry. I took a funny spell. It's been happening quite a lot lately."

Garda Conway nodded sympathetically. "Of course. I imagine it's difficult. Sergeant Brennan and your husband. Did their paths ever cross before?"

"I don't know," she said, shaking her head. "Like I said, I only met Patrick after he decided he was done with that life. They might have. Why are you asking me and not the sergeant?"

"Oh, you know how it is—we deal with so many cases that it's hard to remember all of the people we've come across. I thought you might have been aware of some past thing between the sergeant and your husband. Anyway, we won't keep you any longer. Thank you very much, Mrs Kilcomer."

26

The gravel crunched under their feet as they made their way back to Garda Conway's car.

"So what do you think?" Fi asked.

He shrugged and unlocked the doors remotely. "I don't know. I thought there might be a link. Some history between her husband and Brennan."

"And you don't think so now?"

"If there was she doesn't know about it. Feasible, I suppose. I didn't realise they married such a short time ago."

"Was it not in her file?"

He shook his head. "I told you. There wasn't much detail in there. It sounds like she's singing from the same hymn sheet as Brennan anyway."

"The gang thing."

He nodded.

"But it can't be. We'd have seen them."

He sighed. "That's not the only thing bothering me about this. This was a poisoning. Not very gangland."

She shrugged.

"What if you were a psychologist? One used to dealing with criminals all day every day?"

"Wait, you think it was her?" she gasped, clinging on to the handle above the door as Conway took a roundabout too quickly.

He made a face. "I don't think so. That house is hers. Always was. I did a little digging this morning outside of the sparse notes Brennan has made. She had nothing to gain by murdering him."

"Did anyone?"

"Doesn't sound like it. He didn't have much to his name."

"Officially."

"If he'd cut ties with his gang, he would have had to walk away. I doubt he came away with much. Their money is hers."

"Okay. So it's not the guests and it's not the wife. So who is it then? And why is Brennan so certain it's not a local?"

Garda Conway thought about it for a long while and shook his head. "Only two possibilities that I can see. One, that he has blinkers on his eyes and doesn't want to look past his theory. He can't consider the possibility that the murderer is a local."

"Doesn't sound like him. He always seemed to get off on giving locals a hard time."

"Exactly. So the second theory might be something we need to look at."

"What's that?"

He sighed and shook his head, staring out the windscreen directly in front of him. "That he knows who the killer was and he doesn't want anyone else to find out."

"But who could it be?" Fi asked, throwing up her hands. "I was there and you heard Mrs Kilcomer. She was with him all day. The whole family was. I don't buy this business about a ninja gang member sneaking in unseen and poisoning him. Surely somebody would have noticed a stranger."

"But you were a stranger to them."

"Sure I was. But I was working."

"How were they to know?"

"Because," she said excitedly as she thought of something. "We had those uniforms. I wore one. So did everybody we hired to work the event except for Kate, but she was running around with that silly Bluetooth earpiece stuck in her ear."

"So now we have something," he said thoughtfully. "We had the guests and all the staff in uniform. How likely do you think it is that somebody could have slipped in undetected?"

She shook her head. "Totally unlikely. Because of the uniforms. Maybe they could have fooled us if they were dressed formally, but one of the guests would have seen. A group of fifty? The killer couldn't have gotten to him without passing a lot of people."

"But he did. And we know he did. The lab is certain that the poison was administered in your pub. So," he said, gripping the wheel. "That leaves us with the certainty that it was somebody present in the pub that day."

"And from the way Brennan's been acting, we know it's a local. He's protecting someone and he doesn't want to risk shining the light on another person from Ballycashel in case somebody makes a leap. But why? Why would anyone in Ballycashel have a grudge against an ex-gang member from Dublin?"

"I don't know," he said with a sigh. "All we can do is follow this lead and hope we find out."

THEY FOUND NOTHING. All of the guests were clean—they knew that already from the background checks on the file. And all of the people who'd worked that day turned out clean too. No criminal records. No links to gangs.

"This is hopeless," Fi muttered.

Conway shrugged. "To be honest, I wasn't hopeful that we'd find anything."

"But you agreed it was our best lead."

"I did," he said after a long pause. "There's definitely something going on. I'm certain about that. Brennan wouldn't just change his way of dealing with this thing if it was a normal case. I'm surprised he hasn't hauled you in. Or your sister or mother. And it must be something big if it's stopping him from acting on his petty little grudges."

"But...?"

"But." He cleared his throat. "But having an idea of what's going on and being able to prove it are two very different things. Brennan's no fool. He'll cover himself. He's not foolish enough to look after someone with links to a dangerous criminal. I'm not long off my pension, Fiona. There's a lot to be said for an easy life."

She nodded. "I understand, I suppose. But if we

don't figure it out, how long's he going to keep my pub as a crime scene?"

He shrugged. "I'm sorry, Fiona. I really am."

"Does this mean you're out?"

"I've got to think of my pension. I won't be that man who slaves all his life and then finds himself homeless because he stood by his principles. Principles won't keep the house warm at night or food in the fridge."

She sighed. She could see what he meant. She wondered herself why she'd thrown herself headfirst into this investigation instead of just walking away from everything. "I understand. But will you do one thing for me? See if any of those people have a link to the sergeant."

"I can't go searching his name. Personnel will receive an alert. Otherwise what's stopping people from searching their friends in the force—or their enemies, God forbid. There has to be some sort of control over information."

She nodded and stood to let him out of the house. That was it, it seemed. There was nowhere else to go from there, especially if Conway had decided to put an end to their unofficial investigation.

THE NEXT MORNING, though, Fiona had a renewed sense of purpose. What was she going to do with her days if she couldn't run the pub? Brennan was obviously dragging this thing out for some reason so who knew when she'd be able to reopen?

Well, she wasn't going to let him win.

She tiptoed upstairs and crept into Kate's room to retrieve her sister's laptop. Then she returned to the sitting room and set herself up with a huge pot of tea.

She was going to get to the bottom of this and catch Brennan if it was the last thing she did.

Half an hour later, though, she was staring at the screen in frustration. She'd trawled through countless pages of search results for 'Alex Brennan'. She'd found nothing more than proof that he'd had an extremely privileged upbringing. And she'd already known that.

Next she added 'Kilcomer' to the search. There were pages and pages of results, which made her hopeful for all of the ten seconds it took her to see that they were nonsensical pages full of random names scraped from other parts of the internet.

She sighed. So Brennan and Kilcomer didn't

have an official connection. Brennan hadn't worked on any case against Kilcomer.

Sighing, she drummed her fingers against the laptop and tried to motivate herself. When she started this, she'd been optimistic that there must be something out there. And there was. She just needed to find it.

She ran searches for 'Brennan' and every member of staff that had worked that day.

She was out of ideas.

Finally, bored and needing a break from scanning through random websites with no relevant information, she opened up a new notepad file and began to type everything she knew about Sergeant Brennan.

-*Control freak.*

-*Wealthy father who's a close friend of the Garda Commissioner.*

-*No problem with harassing Ballycashel residents and charging them with minor crimes/questioning them for things they haven't done.*

-*Unfriendly.*

-*Sense of superiority.*

She sighed and shook her head. She really didn't like the man, but that wasn't enough. There had to be something else. And there was. Unrelated, but she supposed it was tied in in one way.

-Corrupt? Associated with Bernard Boyle. Not so squeaky clean after all.

She stared at the screen.

She didn't really believe it was connected, but something compelled her to go back to the browser and type Boyle's name into the search window. She and Garda Conway suspected him of being involved in some sort of corruption with Sergeant Brennan, but they hadn't yet found out what it was the two men were up to.

The search results for Boyle were similar to the ones that had come up for Brennan. Lots of images of fancy functions. She wasn't particularly surprised. He was always dressed to the nines whenever she'd seen him around town. He was that type of guy. Connected.

She froze. *Connected.* What if... It seemed like a ludicrous idea, even to her, but she had nothing else to go on. She typed in Boyle's name and started to look for connections between him and all of the staff members that had worked that day.

By now her stomach was growling and she was getting impatient. It was becoming clear that this was a wild goose chase.

With two names left to go, she considered abandoning her pointless quest, but she kept on. It wasn't like she had anything else to do.

Searching Boyle's name and Tom Kenny returned two pages of results, but there was nothing meaningful in there. It was just like all the other searches: there were results but they looked like directory pages where lists of names had been scraped from other corners of the internet.

She typed in 'Bernard Boyle' and 'Jason Greene' and waited, expecting to see much the same thing.

But she didn't.

This search was different. There were more results and they were more varied. These sites were more legitimate looking and the text in the previews actually made sense rather than simply being a list of random names.

Fiona's heart leapt when she saw that the Sunday Saturn was one of the websites listed in the results. She clicked on the link and scanned impatiently through it as soon as it had loaded.

She'd been expecting something significant and was disappointed to find the first mention of him described him as the secretary of Ballycashel golf club. That wasn't exactly new information. It was just some article about golf.

She was about to give up in disgust when she remembered she hadn't searched Jason's name on the page. What was he doing in an article that seemed to be describing some kind of golf event? He was just some young guy from a nearby town who they'd never seen around Ballycashel.

Searching for Jason brought her to a photo caption. And there he was. Standing beside Bernard Boyle, who had his arm clamped firmly around the young man's shoulders.

Fiona shook her head in disbelief. Was it a coincidence? Not judging from the resemblance between the two men. She shut the laptop and raced upstairs to her sister.

27

"**K**ate!" she cried, throwing open the door and launching herself at her sister's sleeping form. "Wake up! I need to talk to you."

Kate jerked awake with a squeal and then a groan as she realised what had just happened. "Ugh! Why'd you wake me? It's not even eight."

"Jason. Tell me everything you know about him."

"Why? God, Fiona. Can't this wait? I thought you were seeing that Angus guy."

"Just answer the question!" Fiona looked around for something to throw at her sister but resisted the urge. She didn't have time for this.

Kate looked like she was about to say something snappy but restrained herself. "He came to me. He'd heard about the wedding. Offered to work for free to get experience."

"Didn't you think that was weird?"

Kate shrugged. "People work for free all the time. I didn't think anything of it. And he did a good job. It wasn't his fault that somebody got murdered at an event he was working at."

Fiona swallowed and looked away. She didn't want to get into the truth just yet. After all, she wasn't sure. It just seemed a remarkable coincidence, that was all. Was Jason the guy Brennan was protecting?

"Where'd you meet him?"

"He contacted me. Said he lived in Cloher and wanted some work experience. The Kilcomers wanted loads of staff to make the day special and I was having trouble finding people at short notice. So it was perfect. What's this about? Don't tell me you have your knickers in a twist about me bringing in outside help to run your bar."

"It's not. But now that you mention it, why'd you trust the guy? You didn't know him at all and yet you signed him up to work a cash bar."

"He sent me his CV and I had a quick interview with him. Anyway it wasn't your cash I was trusting him with. It was mine."

"So he contacted you out of the blue. An email?"

Kate nodded.

"Can I see it?"

Grumbling, Kate picked up her phone and fumbled with it for a few moments. Then she handed it to Fi. "Don't go breaking this one. I'd to pay a fortune for it."

Fi scanned the email. At first she was frustrated —it was just a perfectly polite enquiry about a job. But then she thought of something. She clicked on the attachment and waited for it to load.

She scrolled through, hoping.

And there it was. 7/6/89.

She assumed he'd used the correct date in case Kate had needed to run police checks. She raced downstairs to call Garda Conway.

HE WAS NOT in a good mood. He just grunted when she told him they had a possible person of interest. He didn't even ask for the name and details.

"Why aren't you more interested?" she asked, frustrated. "I think this is Boyle's son. It can't be a coincidence. It's too much."

He was silent for a few moments. "Brennan just gave me a right hiding over talking to Mrs Kilcomer."

Her first instinct was to console him. After all, she knew how much he wanted to stay under the radar until he could retire and live in peace. Her eyes widened as his words sank in.

"How'd he know? You didn't make a note about our visit, did you?"

He clicked his tongue. "Of course not."

Fiona's heart hammered. "How did he know then?"

"Mrs Kilcomer, I suppose."

"But why? All we did was go there and ask questions about the case. Why would she have called him to tell him that?"

Conway sucked in a breath. "I have to go."

"Wait!" she squealed. "The guy's name is Jason Greene. I have his date of birth."

"I don't need it," he said impatiently. "I already ran police checks on that list of names you gave me. They're all clean."

"But this is new! I found a picture in the paper of him with Boyle. And they look similar. Just check his birth cert. And this thing with Mrs Kilcomer!"

"What thing?" he grunted. "That doesn't prove anything. She might have thought I was a little insensitive is all."

"Please, Garda Conway. Please just look into

Jason's connection to Boyle. They've a different surname but that doesn't mean anything. If he's not a son he could be a nephew."

Conway was silent for a while. Fiona started to think she was fighting a losing battle. But then he sighed. "Fine. Okay. What else have I to do today? Leave it with me."

28

F our days later, Fiona was beginning to regret her insistence. She'd gone to Phelan's every night since they spoke and there'd been no sign of Garda Conway. She'd stopped trying to hide the fact that they were unofficially working on the Kilcomer case—not that the act had made any difference. Jimmy had known what they were up to all along.

He tried to convince her to stop worrying on each of the first three nights when there was no word from Garda Conway. It might be a cold, he said. Or some relation that was sick.

By the fourth evening, though, even Jimmy was worried.

"It's not like him. He's as strong as an ox. He's been coming in here for the past ten years. He's missed a night here and there, but never four in a row."

Fiona felt sick to her stomach. What had she gotten him in to? She'd been trying to call his mobile repeatedly, but it was always switched off. She'd called to his house and there was no-one there.

"What is it you think has happened him?"

But Fi couldn't bring herself to share her fears with someone else and risk them disappearing as well. She hurried out of the bar and rushed to the Garda station, praying that it hadn't closed for the day.

"WHAT ARE YOU DOING HERE?"

"Where's Garda Conway? I need to see him."

"You think I don't see what you're doing? You're trying to push your way into my investigation."

She bit her lip. Her stomach was churning and she felt like confronting him with everything she'd found out, but she held off. It needed to come from somebody else. He could do serious harm to her if he wanted to.

"I'm not. I just want to see Garda Conway about my application for a PI licence."

He sneered. "Do you think I'm going to let you get signed off to go meddling in other peoples' affairs even more than you do already?"

This time, she allowed herself to relish in her dislike of him. She realised she couldn't allow him to suspect she knew what Conway was up to—it might be dangerous for him if she did. "No. Of course you wouldn't. That's why I want to see Conway. He's fair and reasonable."

"And I'm...?" He raised an eyebrow and her dislike for him reached new heights.

If you've hurt Garda Conway...

"I don't even know where to start. Anyway. I don't want to sit here and keep looking at you. Where is he? When'll he be back?"

He waved his hand dismissively. "He's at home sick. Where else do you think he is? Very inconvenient. I'm having to work the desk myself now because Fitzpatrick can't work all day until close, according to the HR people."

She opened her mouth to respond, but he beat her to it.

"Get out of here. Go on. It's bad enough having to work the desk without having to deal with leeches like you."

FIONA WAS at her wit's end. She paced the rooms in her parents' house, desperately trying to think of something. There were his friends who'd met them in Dublin, but she didn't even know their surnames, let alone where to find them. What was the station Conway had worked at before he'd been transferred to Ballycashel? She didn't know that either.

She knew she needed to face facts. Brennan was still at the station. Conway wasn't. Nor was he going to the pub in the evenings. A man like him wouldn't let a dose of the cold get in the way of his evening entertainment. Hadn't Jimmy said he'd only ever missed a day or two here and there? But he *was* older now, maybe things like that affected him more severely now...

She felt a burst of optimism and picked up the landline. A moment later, she was dropping it back in its cradle. Finbarr had just confirmed that yes, Conway was his patient, and no, he hadn't visited him in over a year.

She was about to go back to his house and see if she could find a way in when there was a knock at the door. Fi raced down the hall and threw the door open.

"Granny Coyle!" she muttered, disappointed. "Why didn't you use your key? I've never known you to knock before."

"I'm sorry if I gave you a fright, Fiona. I suppose I'm in a state of shock. I must have forgotten." She shook her head as if she couldn't make out what was going on.

"Granny," Fi cried. "What's wrong?"

"Oh, Fiona. I'm after coming straight from the Garda station."

29

It felt like her stomach had plummeted twenty storeys. Her heart hammered as if she'd just run all the way there from town even though she hadn't left the house for hours.

"What is it, Granny? Come in."

Her granny's walk was usually confident and assured. Now it was nothing like that. She moved aimlessly along the hall and into the kitchen, pausing as if waiting for Fiona to tell her where to go.

Fi didn't like this; didn't like it one bit. It took a lot to rattle her grandmother.

"What happened, Granny?" she cried again, hurrying forward and pulling the woman into a hug. Fi didn't think she'd ever seen her like that before because she was usually so calm.

"Oh, Fiona," she gasped. "You're not going to believe it."

"Try me. It's Garda Conway, isn't it?"

Her granny pulled away and frowned up at her. "No, it's not. It's Brennan. And Boyle. I can't even believe what I just witnessed."

Fi gasped, not allowing herself to hope for the best. "What? What about them?"

"Well they've been rounded up, of course. I was just after getting into Phelan's when Seanie came lumbering in to tell us there were unmarked cars all over the town. Well, we ran as fast as our legs would carry us. I only saw Brennan being dragged out. Not the other fella, but I heard all about it. Apparently Boyle was dragged out of his office at the golf club. They haven't been taken to the station here; they were put in the cars. They must have taken them off to Dublin."

Fi felt around behind her with shaking fingers, groping for a chair. She felt like she might pass out at any moment. "Any sign of Garda Conway?"

Granny Coyle shook her head. "No. There was a crowd gathered around but I saw no sign of him."

She tried everything. She wandered around the town but the Garda station was closed. She went to Phelan's but there was no sign of him. The crime scene tape was still plastered across the outside of her pub. Nothing appeared to have changed. Finally, at ten o'clock when the town was quiet and dormant, she did the only thing she could do. She went back home to her parents' house.

They were all crammed into the living room watching the telly. Fiona sat down with them but she couldn't relax.

"Any word about what happened at the Garda station?"

Her father shushed her. "Stop it, now. If you want to talk will you go out to the kitchen? It's getting to the good bit."

Her granny had gone home so there was nothing for it but to join them and watch in silence, even though she had about a hundred questions swirling around her head.

There was a knock on the door about an hour later. Some of the others had fallen asleep, but Fiona was wide awake, staring at the screen and still wondering what had happened.

She looked around and frowned. They were all there so it wasn't one of her siblings knocking because they'd forgotten to bring their key. Nobody else moved to get up so Fi did. She padded down the hallway to the door and pulled it open.

She gasped when she saw who was there.

"Garda Conway! You're alright! I was worried."

He smiled lopsidedly. "Ah, you shouldn't have worried. I was grand. Very busy is all. Can I come in?"

She led him back down the hall and into the kitchen, where she turned on the kettle and offered him a seat at the table.

"Did you get him? Granny said Brennan was barrelled into the back of a van and so was Boyle."

He nodded, suddenly exhausted looking. "Your hunch was right. Jason Greene is Boyle's son. Even so, that proves nothing but it was odd given Boyle's link to Brennan. I went to Dublin and got a friend to run the checks, just to be on the safe side. I wasn't really expecting anything out of it. In fact, we must have spent two days staring at the screen and trying to work out what the link was."

"And how did you? What was it?"

"We couldn't figure it out."

"Oh," she said, disappointed. "But I thought—"

"We dug deeper. And deeper. I thought I'd go mad thinking about it. And then it came to me.

Kilcomer's wife. You were surprised that she called Brennan to say we'd visited, but I didn't think too much of it. Then I reflected on it. I've had complaints in my time, but it's always been from suspects' families. Victims' families are usually just glad you're trying to get to the truth." He smiled. "Mrs Kilcomer and Brennan are old family friends."

"No! But I searched for links between Brennan and Kilcomer. Nothing came up."

"Did you search under her maiden name?"

She slapped her head. "No, I didn't even think of it. God, so it was right there under our noses all along. But wait, you're saying she's involved? That was the key to this whole thing?"

He smiled. "It was a piece in the puzzle. We knew we were close when we found that. We followed Jason and took him to a location far away from Brennan's or his father's influence."

"And?"

Conway rubbed his face. "This thing is far bigger than anything we had imagined. Jason was all bluster at first, but he soon realised he wasn't going anywhere until he told us what he knew. And what a story it turned out to be. He didn't know all of it, of course, but we were able to figure out the rest from what he could tell us. We searched his house and found the poison. He confessed. He did it."

"I don't believe it."

"It gets worse. It's not just Brennan and Boyle. It's far bigger than that. There's a network of them. All connected through family, having gone to college together, that sort of thing. This is huge, Fiona."

"So who wanted Kilcomer dead? And where does his wife come into all of this if Jason did it?"

Garda Conway shook his head. "This is the most difficult part to believe. It was her. Jason poisoned her, but it was at her request."

Fi gasped. "No!"

Conway nodded. "It seems her husband's enthusiasm to stay out of his old life was starting to wane. It wasn't just his desire to throw a big wedding with all his old pals. It was other things. She found out he'd been trying to get in contact with old acquaintances in the south of Spain. She couldn't handle it. It was bad enough that she'd been made a laughing stock when they first got together. Now he was refusing to play ball and act like any other husband in her circle. Her remaining friends would have run a mile from her if they'd found out."

"So she got them to kill him?"

"But I still don't get it. How did it all come together?"

"It'll take us a while to unravel exactly what went on. But we believe we're looking at a network that's been operating for years. Twenty, thirty individuals in the position to smooth things for their friends when needed. Maybe even more people. They dealt in favours, planning permission, that sort of thing. Even murder, it seems."

Fiona shivered. "But how? It's all just too coincidental. Kate only launched her business a few months ago."

"Your sister opening her wedding business was the perfect opportunity for them, but if she hadn't opened the business they'd have found another way no doubt. All Mrs Kilcomer needed to do was throw money at her step-daughter and pressure her to get married quickly. Boyle enlisted his son—different surname, so it would have been difficult for him to be traced back even in the unlikely event Boyle was implicated. All he had to do was get a job at the bar. It was Mrs Kilcomer who suggested to your sister that they wanted very attentive service. Then Jason's email appeared so of course she was willing to take him on when he was offering to work for free. Brennan was on hand to make sure the investigation never got anywhere. It was easy for him to take the glass that had been used to poison Kilcomer—he was there before the crime scene team even showed up. Then all he had to do was steer the thing away from Jason and delay the investigation for long enough that everyone eventually lost interest. Smoke and mirrors. It's clear now why he never made a note of Kilcomer's gang connections. That would have drawn attention."

"Wow," Fiona gasped, shaking her head. All of this had been mainly speculation on their part and they'd spent months trying to figure out what was going on between Brennan and Bernard Boyle. Now they knew. "Why would he risk his career for this?"

Conway smiled. "He hasn't risked his career. Fiona, this isn't some new thing. It's been going on for as long as Brennan's been in the guards. It was perfect, you see. As the son of one of the commissioner's best friends, he was above questioning. Even if anyone suspected him, they'd need an iron-clad reason to go up against him. His by-the-book act was another shield against ever being found out."

"But I don't understand! He's a boring nightmare. You're telling me he faked that?"

"No indeed," Garda Conway murmured. "I

happen to agree with you. He was dull and petty. But he was also corrupt to the core."

"What's going to happen to him now?"

"Well for now he's being charged with accessory to murder. The financial team are working through to see just how far back this goes and how widely they've spread their influence, but it's looking like a major scandal."

"Has he been fired?"

Conway laughed. "Not even a man with Brennan's connections could survive a scandal like this."

"Oh. Wow."

He nodded. "Yeah. So it looks like his reign over Ballycashel is over at last."

"Unless they get someone even worse as sergeant."

Surprisingly he didn't try to persuade her otherwise. He just smiled and drank his tea.

30

F iona soon found out just why Garda Conway was so relaxed about getting another monster as a boss.

The powers that be had already decided who would be the new sergeant for the town.

Sergeant Stephen Conway.

The appointment was only announced once the dust began to settle on the scandal of Sergeant Brennan and his friends. At first Brennan would say nothing to the investigators, but he finally caved when it became clear to him that even his father's connections couldn't save him now.

It was plain old greed. He and Boyle had gone to university with Mrs Kilcomer and they'd all been part of a bigger group of wealthy young professionals from affluent families who had associated with each other for generations.

They'd helped each other out; done favours for each other over the years. Brennan had apparently tried to get out of it once or twice, but by that stage, the group's grip on him was too strong. By then, they had video evidence of him accepting money in brown envelopes in exchange for favours.

It was often silly little things. Look the other way for this. Provide signoff for a dodgy passport. Say you were with someone when you weren't. But when they asked him to look the other way when a murder was committed, he still didn't really bat an eyelid. As far as he was concerned, the man was scum who deserved it anyway.

Mrs Kilcomer had helped pay off Bernard Boyle's gambling debts several years before, so of course there was no question of him agreeing to help her with a little problem. It wasn't the first time one of them had facilitated a murder either.

They were never found because there was no official organisation. Just a bunch of wealthy friends looking out for each other. Until it had taken a sinister turn.

They finally found out why Brennan had received a brown envelope from Boyle. It was to do with a planning application on Boyle's land. Brennan had greased the palms of another friend in the planning department and succeeded in getting approval for a luxury development.

Which would now never be built.

"Good God," Margaret McCabe muttered when her husband was finished reading the update on the case from that day's paper. "Is there anyone honest in this world anymore? I knew he was obnoxious, but this is unbelievable."

"Well he'll get his comeuppance. They're not letting this go. And it sounds like Garda Conway is some kind of hero to them. Sergeant Conway. I never thought he was bothered about promotion."

"Maybe they made him an offer he couldn't refuse," Fiona said with a smile, thinking she couldn't imagine anyone more deserving of the job.

"Let's hope things calm down now in Bally-cashel," her mother said, finishing her tea and standing up to take their plates away.

"So you're staying put then?" Francis muttered, looking straight at Fi when he said it.

"Of course! Why would you ask?"

"I heard you were a bit fidgety. Thinking of running off when things got too much."

She shrugged defensively. "No. It crossed my mind but I didn't. How'd you even know?"

He tapped the side of his nose. "I pay more attention than I let on."

Of course he did. She should have known. There wasn't a lot that went on in that house that escaped Francis McCabe's notice.

He watched her over the top of his newspaper. "So you're staying put?"

She thought about it and smiled. "Of course. Where else would I go?"

31

Mrs Flanagan was practically unrecognisable on the day of Marie's wedding. Between Kate and Fi, they'd found a manor house about twenty miles away that had just had another function cancelled.

A lot of the guests had already booked their accommodation at B&Bs in the town, so Kate arranged buses to ferry them back to Ballycashel. The bride, her family and her new husband's family were delighted to stay at the manor house.

Still, both Kate and Fi were a bit apprehensive about seeing the indomitable Mrs Flanagan again.

They needn't have been.

She pulled them aside after the first dance and dragged them to the bar to have a champagne with her. Fi thought they were going to get an ear-bashing at first, but only before she saw the soft look in the woman's eyes.

"I wanted to thank you both. For your discretion."

Fi glanced at her sister and shrugged. "No worries. We promised we wouldn't say anything. And you're my sister's client after all."

"Ye must have thought I was an awful demanding aul bag."

Fi bit the insides of her cheeks. "Weddings are stressful. Especially when it's your daughter getting married. It's understandable."

Mrs Flanagan narrowed her eyes. "Don't give me that. I know what I was like. I let myself get swept up in the same sort of thing that Fintan's friends' wives were all at. I see that now. It's no wonder Marie wanted a small little wedding. She only told me this morning—she was worried I'd invite all my awful friends and make a scene."

Kate shook her head and clasped the woman's arm. "Would you go away out of that?"

"It's true," Mrs Flanagan said firmly. "I'm sorry you had to witness it. I've a lot of apologies to make in the next few weeks." She took a large swig of her champagne. "I suppose I was so afraid of Pa that I immersed myself completely in my husband's world. I don't even know myself anymore."

Kate looked bewildered by this. Fi reckoned she knew why. It didn't sound like Mrs Flanagan was very happy in her life anymore and it was hardly a good advertisement for a wedding planner that she'd caused her client's parents to divorce.

Mrs Flanagan must have seen her panic. "Oh, don't you worry now. I'm not doing anything mad. It's not my husband who's the snob. It's a lot of the women in his circle. Fintan is about as down to earth as it's possible to get. His mother on the other hand..."

"Phew," Fiona said when Mrs Flanagan had left them to go and chat with some of the guests. "For a moment there I thought we were after causing tensions in her marriage. It wouldn't be a very good thing for your business."

Kate tossed her hair back. "Doesn't matter, Fi. I think I'm kind of over wedding planning. It's a lot of work."

"What? But you were all into it! You've set up your website! And you looked like you were about to have a heart attack when it seemed like Mrs Flanagan was on about leaving her husband."

"Ah no," Kate said waving her hand. "What do you think I am? I wasn't worried about my business. It was more that I didn't want to see her do anything drastic. She's a nice woman now she's dropped the whole snobbery thing."

"I didn't know you were that soft."

Kate shook her head and smiled. "You didn't see her that day I went to their house before you showed up. She was so upset. You couldn't not feel for her after seeing her that way."

"My God," Fi gasped in mock shock. "So you do have a heart. Who'd have thought it?"

"Very funny," Kate said, pulling a face. "This is awkward, but I also wanted to thank you for helping me with the business."

"It's no problem," Fi said, pulling her into a hug that felt extremely awkward. Because even though they were sisters, they weren't exactly what anyone might call close. She pulled away as soon as possible. "So you're serious? You're really calling it quits on the wedding planning business? I thought this was something you might stick at long-term."

"Nah. It's a nightmare, to be honest. You remember the Clancy wedding?"

"Of course I do. It was only a few days ago." They'd gotten the pub back and had gone crazy cleaning the place and returning the hired crockery and glasses that were by then more than a week overdue to be returned to the hire company. Then they'd spent hours decorating the place, setting up the tables and doing all the prep work for the meal. Fiona remembered it alright. It was the busiest she'd ever been in her life.

"And?" Kate demanded.

Fi shrugged. "It was busy. But it's done now."

"It was painful! I thought wedding planning was all about getting everything set up in advance so there was no need to get stressed out on the day. I hadn't planned on it being one disaster after another. So many things went wrong! Not so much with that wedding, but with finding a whole new venue for this one."

"So? That's what event planning is all about. Why'd you think people give you all that money? It's not because they think you've got great taste. It's so you'll do all the hard work and they won't have to."

"Mmm," Kate said, knocking back the rest of her champagne. "Well I've learned my lesson. I'm not moving from the couch for the rest of the month. Then I'm going to find something to do that's relaxing and doesn't require me to run around the place like a madwoman."

Fiona smiled. She should have known that her sister would soon run out of enthusiasm for the venture. There had been no point in pushing her, but she was glad there'd be no middle of the night phone calls from Kate looking for her help in setting something up.

Just as she thought that, of course, Granny Coyle bolted over to them. Kate had enlisted her to help behind the makeshift bar they'd set up in the corner of the grand drawing room of the manor house. It wasn't one of those places that had been turned into a bar and restaurant. This was an old house that hadn't been renovated in years that the owners sometimes hired out for events to make a bit of extra cash.

"That's it," Rose said mutinously. "I'm done."

"What happened, Granny? I thought you liked helping and having the chats with a load of random people."

She glared at Fiona. "I do not. And don't think I'm just going to forget about our business idea. Has there been any word from Garda Conway about the Private Investigator licence? Did you think you could just not mention it and I'd forget?"

Fi shook her head. The truth was she'd been so busy over the past several weeks that she hadn't given the matter any thought at all.

Setting up their own private investigations business had been her grandmother's idea, which Fi had gone along with half-heartedly, but the process for getting licensed to operate was anything but straightforward. She'd secretly been glad when they'd lodged their applications and then heard nothing back at all.

"It's probably because we have no experience as actual private investigators, Granny."

"It's not. Sure haven't we helped out with a load of murder cases?"

"Shhh. Keep your voice down. We're at a wedding."

"I know we are. Don't I have champagne spilled all over me."

Kate groaned. "I've got stuff to do. You two can fight this out amongst yourselves." She turned and disappeared into the crowd.

When Fi looked back at her grandmother, the old woman's scowl was gone. In its place was a wide, mischievous smile.

"What are you up to?" Fi asked, frowning. "I thought you were mad at me."

"Not at all. I just wanted to get rid of her for a while and take a break. These people are mad for the drink. I haven't been able to take a breath since this thing started."

Fi nodded. She knew what Granny Coyle meant. She'd been on waitressing duties and her feet were aching from running around the place. "Did you hear? Kate's not interested in setting up any more weddings."

"Glory be is all I can say. I'm not able for all this at my age."

"But you're still mad to set up an investigations business."

Granny Coyle nodded, eyes alight with enthusiasm. "I am. I know the licence takes a while; I was only talking about it to get Kate off our backs for a while. She's not in my good books at the moment after making me wear this stupid yoke."

All the bar staff were in sober black waistcoats for the event, and Granny Coyle had taken against hers in a major way.

"Ah, I thought you looked nice in it. A bit like a dotty old lady who got dressed from the wrong side of the wardrobe by mistake."

Rose swiped her arm. "Careful. Or I'll have to

find myself someone else to partner with for this business of ours."

"Why are you so keen on private eyeing? You've hated every moment of helping Kate out with the wedding business. They're both service industries."

Rose's eyes narrowed. "These wedding guests are very demanding."

"So are clients in general."

"Dead bodies aren't," Rose said with a grin.

Fiona shuddered. "Good God, Granny. I thought the whole aim of starting our own investigations business was to take on insurance work and track down scammers. You can't say Ballycashel hasn't already had its fair share of murders for one lifetime."

But Granny Coyle would only shrug. "I don't know. I don't know what's going on in the world these days where it's not safe to walk down the street without something happening to you. All I can say is, we might as well take advantage of it and earn ourselves a bit of easy cash."

Fiona shook her head in disbelief.

"What? It's true!"

"We're at a wedding, Granny. You can't say things like that."

"Sure I can say what I want. Anyway, the main

reason I wanted to find you was I've managed to hide a bottle of eighteen-year-old Jameson. Want to come and help me drink it?"

Fi raised an eyebrow.

"Come on. Your sister's paying for it. Do you really think we'll see a penny of the money she's promised us?"

Fiona thought about it. Probably not. It was highly likely that Kate would go off and spend their money on makeup palettes and foreign holidays. That was Kate all over.

"Come on so. We might as well get something out of this debacle."

22220669R00153

Printed in Poland
by Amazon Fulfillment
Poland Sp. z o.o., Wrocław